BRIGHT YOUNG THINGS

Also by Jane A. Adams from Severn House

The Naomi Blake mysteries

MOURNING THE LITTLE DEAD
TOUCHING THE DARK
HEATWAVE
KILLING A STRANGER
LEGACY OF LIES
SECRETS
GREGORY'S GAME
PAYING THE FERRYMAN
A MURDEROUS MIND
FAKES AND LIES

The Rina Martin mysteries

A REASON TO KILL
FRAGILE LIVES
THE POWER OF ONE
RESOLUTIONS
THE DEAD OF WINTER
CAUSE OF DEATH
FORGOTTEN VOICES

The Henry Johnstone mysteries

THE MURDER BOOK
DEATH SCENE
KITH AND KIN
THE CLOCKMAKER
THE GOOD WIFE
OLD SINS

BRIGHT YOUNG THINGS

Jane A. Adams

SEVERN
HOUSE

First world edition published in Great Britain and the USA in 2021
by Severn House, an imprint of Canongate Books Ltd,
14 High Street, Edinburgh EH1 1TE.

Trade paperback edition first published in Great Britain and the USA in 2022
by Severn House, an imprint of Canongate Books Ltd.

severnhouse.com

British Library Cataloguing-in-Publication Data
A CIP catalogue record for this title is available from the British Library.

ISBN-13: 978-0-7278-5013-3 (cased)
ISBN-13: 978-1-78029-803-0 (trade paper)
ISBN-13: 978-1-4483-0541-4 (e-book)

Typeset by Palimpsest Book Production Ltd.,
Falkirk, Stirlingshire, Scotland.
Printed and bound in Great Britain by
TJ Books, Padstow, Cornwall.

393000064l2554

Prologue

No doubt, he thought, there was a word for what he was and what he did. For a man who understood right and wrong and even subscribed to what might be called a moral code, but veered so far away from that when it suited him. And felt no regret at doing so.

Most of his acquaintances would have declared him to be a gentleman, a good sort, decent. A hero even, in certain circles. The fact was that he was capable of heroic and even selfless acts – though were they selfless? Or were they just the result of this damned restless energy that possessed him. This need to push himself so far beyond what any man would reckon normal.

He had no doubt that his father had known what he was and had even understood him on some level or other. Though his father had been a genuinely kind man, a good man and had taught his son that when you were in a position of strength you should reach back and give others a hand up. And he had absorbed that lesson and continued his father's work because he could see the sense in that philosophy. A man well thought of could do the unthinkable and think the unspeakable and win against the odds in circumstances others could not even conceive of, in the sure and certain knowledge that he would never be suspected. Not him. He's a good egg, a solid, cricket playing, upstanding example of English manhood.

The thought amused him.

He stood close to the fireplace and studied the letters she had written to him. This last one. He had read and re-read them so many times now, enjoying the memories, the faint scent of her that clung to the pages. Perfume and powder and girlish softness; that was what she had really been about.

He remembered them all, of course. All different, all presenting another challenge. The chase, the capture, the destruction – over time. He did not like the game to be over too fast. He liked to study his subjects, both in the wild, as it were, and then in captivity. He liked to guess how they might behave; he would have put them under the microscope had that been possible. They added to his collection of slides, of course, but not presented in a way that would give anyone a clue.

He read the letter again, enjoying the moment and the memory, the feeling of power and exultation before the inevitable flatness and ennui.

> I love you. I love you for your kindness and your laughter and the way you make me feel so special and so adored. I love you for the way you look at me, the way you want to know everything about me, the way you make me laugh and even the way you make me cry when I can't see you for days. I want always to be there with you, to laugh and to cry and to enjoy your company and dance with you and go walking as we did that day. You make me so happy.

He knew which of them had written this, of course. The last one in a long, long line, but truthfully it could have been any of them. The same words said, the same overweening and overwhelming and overblown emotion. Did they really think that he was the answer to all of their prayers?

He supposed he was. For a little time.

The only annoyance was that he had not retrieved his own letters this time, the ones sent to her. He told them always to be discreet and destroy their correspondence, but of course they never did. It was too, too precious. Too wonderful. Too sublime. Usually he managed to retrieve his letters once the game was over, but there had been no opportunity this time and he didn't know what she might have done with them.

Of course, it was possible that she'd actually followed his instructions and cast them into the fire. Somehow he doubted that.

It wasn't that he was in any way concerned about others finding them. The handwriting was not his own and they were signed always with a single initial – that wasn't his either. No, it was that he must now go to the trouble of having more letters written, ready for the next time, though he supposed that he'd had his money's worth. This batch of correspondence had done service for him on three – or was it four? – occasions now.

Should he burn the letters she had written to him?

No, not yet. There was still more enjoyment left in them. He would keep them for a little time. Perhaps until the game began again.

ONE

December had been wet and windy along the south coast with storms blowing in off the sea and winds reaching sixty miles per hour further along the coast. January had dawned, still wet though not unseasonably cold. Even so, the early morning of Sunday, January the fifth, people kept their heads down as they headed for church and didn't even bother to put up their umbrellas, knowing they would soon be blown inside out.

At eight thirty in the morning it was still not fully light. Leaden grey skies, though enlivened by a few rebelliously scudding clouds, gave the impression that full daylight was never really going to arrive and that the inhabitants of Bournemouth would have to make do with light levels more reminiscent of dusk. The handful of people hurrying along the promenade became aware of a solitary figure walking along on the shoreline, just above the reach of the mud-brown waves. He appeared to be holding a bundle in his arms and now he turned to face the promenade and stood still as though waiting for someone to notice him. Such was his stillness and the size of him – tall and broad – and the fact that the bundle he held seemed to resolve itself into a body once you had paused and looked at him properly, it was hard not to give him the attention he obviously craved. He drew level with a group of people on the promenade. They had stopped and were now pointing and staring at him. Once one of those had run off, obviously in search of a constable, he laid his burden down on the ground and walked away as unhurriedly as if he had been out for a Sunday stroll. He seemed absurdly certain that the little knot of people on the promenade would not approach him until the constable arrived, and as it happened he was right. The two men and their wives, along with three small children, did not go down on to the beach, though they watched anxiously as the waves pulled and tugged at what was now obviously a body on the beach. The man seemed to have engendered an almost superstitious awe; what normal person stood on the beach with a body until noticed and then calmly put it down and walked away? This action displayed all the signs of insanity, perhaps even murderous insanity, and overrode the concern of one of the women that whoever was lying on the sand might simply be injured and in need of help.

She was about to insist that her husband, Mr Colin Chambers, should go down and at least take a look, when her younger brother, who had run off in search of a constable, returned with the same. Constable Jones, Colin Chambers and his young brother-in-law, Brian Housman, then all went down to the shoreline and it was immediately obvious to the constable that this was no commonplace situation.

The girl lying with her body now soaked by the water was young, perhaps in her early twenties, and she was dressed in a beaded cocktail gown so heavily embellished that it sparkled even in the lowlight. Her hair was now too wet to discern the style, but a bright clip sparkled just above one ear and held in place a sparkling, feather-trimmed band. She wore only one patent leather shoe but the second was close by and had obviously fallen from her foot when the man had carried her. Incongruously a silver evening bag formed of fine maille links was tied to her wrist with a rough piece of bailing twine as though to ensure that it did not get lost.

And although no one could see any marks upon the body, she was very, very dead.

The details of the finding were so extraordinary as to excite the immediate attention of the local newspapers, though of course it was too late for them to do anything about it until the Monday edition. By then even some of the nationals, intrigued by the strange tale the witnesses had told, had picked it up. On the Tuesday afternoon, Henry Johnstone, drinking tea in his sister's front parlour, two streets back from the promenade, read the latest report with mild interest. He read about the man standing on the shoreline with the body in his arms, making sure that he was noticed. He read about the way the woman was dressed, as though she had just left a party and he read that she had been taken to a nearby funeral directors. Like everybody else who read the reports, he pondered as to who this young woman might be and felt a mild irritation that no one had given chase when the mysterious man, tall and broad though he might have been, had dumped her body on the beach.

No, Henry thought, if the report was to be believed, that was not what happened. This mysterious man had *placed* the body carefully, ceremoniously and deliberately. Had he just dropped it and run, then it was likely someone would have given chase. It was the very strangeness and deliberateness of his actions that had given everyone pause; that had filled them with disquiet. He pondered on this for a moment or two and then moved on to other news items. This was not his concern. A few short weeks ago, of course, it might have been, but Henry had not yet decided whether he would go back to work, even though he had now been reinstated as a detective chief inspector working out of the Central Office in New Scotland Yard. A murder detective working with the murder squad.

Henry dropped the paper on to a side table and paced the room restlessly, wondering whether he should go out for a walk. You are getting lazy, Henry Johnstone, he told himself. The injury to his shoulder was healed now, though his shoulder was still painful and stiff and his left arm only partially useful. He had been told that it would improve and that he must move it, exercise it gently and gradually increase the strain he put upon it, but he had been less than assiduous. He had come to realize that he was not sure he wanted to recover, that fullness of recovery meant he would have to leave his sister's house and go back into the world and face the dangers there, and Henry, in his more honest moments, was not certain he was ready for that.

He heard a car pull up outside the house but took little notice of it. It was the sound of his niece, Melissa, thirteen years old and now squealing excitedly and running down the stairs that alerted him to the fact that this car brought a visitor.

'Uncle Henry, Uncle Henry, it's Mickey,' Melissa shouted excitedly as she passed the maid in the hall and opened the door herself. Henry went out into the hall and was greeted by the sight of Mickey hugging Melissa enthusiastically, a rather embarrassed-looking police driver standing behind him. A second later he noticed that Mickey had a suitcase at his feet but still clasped in his right hand was another bag, one Henry knew well: the murder bag, equipped with all they would need to search a crime scene and to investigate a crime.

Mickey turned to the driver and gave him instructions to come back first thing in the morning, checking that he had organized accommodation for the night. He looked up at Cynthia, Henry's sister, who, attracted by the noise, now stood on the stairs with a broad smile on her face.

'Mickey, my love, come along in. Never a more welcome sight.' She came down the stairs, took his free hand and he kissed her on the cheek. Henry was struck for a moment by the difference between these three people he loved. Melissa, young, her red hair bright and her pretty features so much like her mother's. Cynthia poised, beautifully coiffed and expensively dressed. Sergeant Mickey Hitchens, neat and scrubbed, his hair a steely grey and his face lined and a little crumpled; his heavy overcoat of dog-tooth check was new to Henry but he guessed that Mickey or his wife Belle would have found it at the second-hand market, Belle having an eye for good cloth and for a good bargain. His heavy boots were well polished but also well worn. A man come prepared to work and, Henry realized with a jolt, a man come to fetch his boss out of his temporary retirement.

The police driver obviously did not know Cynthia, or Henry's relationship to this obviously wealthy woman, hence his look of disquiet when he had dropped Mickey off and his further look of uncertainty, cast back before he got into the car.

'For goodness' sake, close the front door before we all catch a chill. Biddy, bring tea, please.'

'Yes ma'am.' The maid grinned at Henry, and then at Mickey, as though Mickey Hitchens' arrival was excellent news even below stairs. Not that there was a hell of a lot of differentiation in *this* house, Henry thought.

Then Cynthia's eye was caught by the bag Mickey held and she took a step back. 'You're here on business,' she said. 'You're here to get Henry.'

'And I'm here to impose on your hospitality if you'll have me,' Mickey told her.

'You are welcome as spring,' Cynthia told him but Henry could see the anxious look in her eye now. They had both known that this day would come, when Henry could not put off his decision any longer. Would he go back to his role as detective, would he decide to turn away? Here, in Cynthia's hallway, decision time had arrived and Henry knew, just looking at his sergeant's face, that it had been made for him. Mickey was here; his oldest and dearest friend was here asking for help. Mickey had never let Henry down and Henry was not about to do so either.

'Is it about that woman on the beach?' Melissa wanted to know. 'Do they know who she is yet?'

'Melissa, you are supposed to be attending to your lessons,' Cynthia told her gently. 'You can pester Mickey all you like later.'

Melissa knew the tone of her mother's voice and that it was pointless to argue. They watched as she went back upstairs and then adjourned to the front parlour. Mickey stood warming his hands in front of the fire, the murder bag dumped somewhat incongruously beside the fire irons. Henry said, 'It's good to see you. Whatever the circumstances, it's good to see you.'

He had met with Mickey briefly over the Christmas holiday, visiting Mickey and Belle at their home, but that had been the last time. The longest they had ever been apart in years had been these past weeks, since Henry had been injured and had moved to his sister's house in Bournemouth to recuperate. Cynthia and her family had recently moved there permanently after selling their London house. Mickey had, in the meantime, been assigned as bagman to one detective or another, settling nowhere.

'You're looking well,' Mickey said, sounding satisfied. 'And Melissa, how is she? Looking better too, I thought.'

Late the year before Melissa had been kidnapped and held by a man who wanted revenge against Henry and who had been quite prepared to kill the child. This had also led to Henry's injury.

'She's recovering,' Cynthia told him. 'We still have bad nights from time to time and there are some days when she just wants to cry, and so I let her, but she will recover, Mickey. We all will.'

Mickey nodded. Biddy arrived with tea and cake and small sandwiches. 'Cook says she knows it's a while until dinner, ma'am, so she thought Sergeant Hitchens might be hungry.'

'Tell Cook thank you. That was a good thought,' Cynthia said.

Henry watched as Biddy nodded happily and went out, closing the door softly behind her. 'It seems my entire household has missed you, Mickey Hitchens,' Cynthia said. 'And I for one am glad you're here. I'm only sorry that it is because some young woman has lost her life. Henry has to get back on the wagon at some time and even though he feels he's not ready, I know that he is.'

'Henry can speak for himself, you know,' Henry said. 'And it *is* good to see you.'

He watched as Mickey filled his plate with sandwiches and cake and Cynthia set his tea on the small occasional table beside the wingback chair. The big overcoat had been taken away and Henry could now see that Mickey was sporting a rather snazzy waistcoat. This had definitely not been bought second-hand and was a deep red. He wondered if it had been a Christmas present from Belle. A watch chain hung from a buttonhole and Henry could just glimpse the top of Mickey's old brass watch peeking out of the waistcoat pocket. It was about time it had a better home, Henry thought, battered though it was and rubbed smooth by years of handling and a life in Mickey's jacket. It had belonged to Mickey's father and had travelled all the way through the First World War, been loved all the years after.

'Do we know who she is?' Henry asked.

Mickey finished a sandwich before replying and then said,

'Ah now, that is where the strangeness lies.' He reached for the murder bag, opened it and took a Manila envelope from inside, handed it to Henry. Then he turned to Cynthia and said, 'I suspect you might know the young woman found on the beach. You and she probably moved in the same circles from time to time. I would not want to upset you, my dear.'

As Henry knew she would, Cynthia came over to sit by him on the small sofa, so she could see the photographs. They had presumably been taken at the funeral directors, the dark panelling and heavy furniture an odd contrast to the woman's body laid out on a table, plain white sheets or perhaps even a tablecloth beneath her.

'There was no chance to take photographs on the beach because of the tide, but fortunately Mr Jamieson, the undertaker, had the presence of mind to take some pictures before she was taken away to the mortuary. He also had the presence of mind to record certain features of the body which seemed peculiar, such as the bag tied to her hand.'

Henry was suddenly aware that Mickey was regarding Cynthia closely and that Cynthia had gasped and was now holding a hand over her mouth as though in shock. 'You do know her?' he asked.

'I do, but it isn't possible – I went to her memorial service last year. Her name, is, was . . . Mickey, it's the same girl but surely that isn't possible. This looks like Faun Moran. But she was killed in a car crash. I saw where she had been interred.'

Mickey shook his head. 'You saw someone buried; it certainly wasn't the unfortunate Miss Moran. Identification in her evening bag indicated that this was indeed Faun Moran and of course the initial reaction was simply that this girl had that young lady's possessions. But the photographs were sent to Central Office, and we compared the face with those images we had on record and the faces certainly matched. We had fingerprints taken and sent to us and they too matched.'

'Why would her fingerprints be on file?' Henry asked.

'Faun was something of a wild child.' It was Cynthia who

replied. 'I believe she was arrested for shoplifting. It was a stupid, wilful thing to do. She had money to pay but it seems she saw stealing as something of an adventure.'

'One of the bright young things who see themselves above the law,' Mickey said, 'or so I've been told.' He looked at Cynthia for confirmation or denial and she nodded.

'Faun was not *wicked* but she was thoughtless and restless and always chafing against what she saw as restrictions. But Mickey, how could she have been found on the beach? Who did I see buried?'

'That, my dear, is our mystery to solve.'

Henry flicked through the photographs. He could see no obvious marks on the body but the head was at a curious angle, the neck hidden by a scarf. 'Was her neck broken?'

'It was; death would have been instantaneous. There were no other injuries on the body.'

Henry paused at a photograph which showed her hand and arm and the bag tied to the wrist. It was impossible to make out what kind of string had been used from the photograph; it looked like ordinary twine, heavier perhaps than might be used to tie a parcel. He looked back at the other photographs. The scarf still in place around the girl's neck, the ornate headband tied around her hair and held in place by the little clip above her ear.

It was Cynthia who voiced the question he had been about to ask. 'It's pretty obvious somebody tied her bag to her wrist so that it didn't get lost, or perhaps to dissuade any common thief who came along and saw something of value. The knot would at least slow them down, I suppose. But why not take the scarf from her neck or tie the bag with the headband – either would have done the job. It looks as though whoever left her body there didn't want to disturb her clothing in any way. Didn't want to give, I don't know, the wrong impression?'

'I'm sure those are Henry's thoughts exactly.' Mickey laughed. 'They were certainly mine.'

Henry nodded brief acknowledgement and then he said, 'According to the newspaper reports I have read, witnesses reckon the man stood there until he was noticed. He didn't want to risk the body being left undiscovered on the beach or washed out to sea. He waited until someone saw him, then he put the body down and walked away. Does that accord with the witness statements?'

'It does indeed. The witnesses were two couples, with their children, and the younger brother of one of the women went to fetch the constable. They say that they saw the man walking along the beach with the bundle in his arms, and that he was glancing towards the promenade. There were others on the promenade but they seemed not to notice him. It was when he drew level with the couples, though he was still some distance away down on the beach, that he stopped and looked directly at them as though wishing to attract their attention. They were walking quite slowly because the children were small. They had come out early for the nine o'clock Mass and as the children had not had a decent walk for a few days they decided to take them along and put up with the fact that meant a slow journey along the promenade. So, this man sees them, he stops, he turns and they realize that he has something in his arms that is not just a bundle. That it's a body. He makes no move to hide the fact, the woman is not wrapped in anything. He made sure he was seen, he watched as the younger brother ran off for the constable. Then he set the body down and he walked away. Walked, mind, he did not run. He was in no hurry.'

'And no one challenged him?' Cynthia asked.

'Bear in mind these are two couples, with three small children in tow. They knew that a constable was being summoned and apparently the man was large, tall and heavyset. But I suspect, from what they have said in the witness statements, that it was also his attitude that dissuaded them. One of the women from the couples said that he behaved like a madman, while the other said that he looked self-assured, as though he could handle himself and didn't care about being approached. They both gained the impression that it would come off badly for anyone who did choose to challenge him.'

'And yet he was determined that the body should be seen and found quickly, and that she should be found with her possessions intact and with as little damage done to the body by the elements as was possible,' Henry mused. 'That I find interesting.'

'It speaks to me of a guilty conscience,' Mickey said.

'Or of love,' Cynthia suggested. 'He cared about her, he wanted her found, and he wanted to have her found by the right people, not by people who would rob her after death.'

'Then why not take her back to her family?' Henry suspected both Mickey and Cynthia might be right, but if the man had cared for her, had felt his conscience pricked, then why leave her on the beach at all.

'Why indeed,' Mickey agreed. 'And who did Faun's family bury? The body was burnt beyond recognition and the young man driving the car has been in a very expensive nursing home ever since. His family have insisted he is not fit to be questioned by anyone, though of course we are working to circumvent that.'

'Malcolm Everson,' Cynthia said. 'His name is Malcolm Everson and he's a nice chap, a little older than the Moran girl. She was not yet twenty. I heard he was in such deep shock that he's barely spoken since. Just imagine what this news will do to him.'

'How can he not have known that Faun Moran was not the woman in his car?' Henry wanted to know.

'Well, there was certainly a lot of gossip about it at the time. It was at the Belmonts' place, you know, up near Matlock. I didn't go up that weekend. It was the younger family members who organized this one and I'm a little long in the tooth and poor in the purse by the standard of all the bright young things they invite to their weekenders. But I have visited on a number of occasions. The Belmonts are nice people and not as stuffy as some, despite being worth a bundle. From what I've been told she certainly got into his car at the start of the journey. They'd been at a party, some kind of charity do, if I remember correctly, and he'd had a few to drink. His friends tried to stop him, but you know how young men are sometimes. He took a bend too fast, the car turned over, he was thrown clear and found unconscious, but the car burst into flames and everyone assumed, naturally, that the body they found was Faun's.'

'And were his injuries consistent with the crash?' Henry asked.

'I've read the accident reports,' Mickey told him, 'and there are copies in the bag so you can take a look yourself. They crashed close to a local farm. The farmer heard the noise of the car as it came round the bend, and he heard it as it came off the road and crashed through the trees. By the time he got there it was well ablaze and from its final position they suspect it must have rolled over two or three times on the way down the hill. The young man's body was found some distance from the car with broken ribs, a broken arm and head injuries. He didn't regain consciousness for several days, and when he did he had a brain fever, was delirious and couldn't remember a thing. Of course, everyone blamed him for the accident. He was most certainly drunk, and the inquest found against him. But the coroner recorded misadventure and the Moran family decided not to bring legal action. I suppose they consider the boy has suffered enough.'

Cynthia frowned. 'That surprised everyone. Caius Moran is not a man to be crossed. Everyone says he rules his family with a rod of iron, which is why I think Faun was so rebellious. Her brother and sister appear to have toed the line, but she was the youngest and the youngest child often gets away with more, I suppose.'

Henry decided to backtrack a little. 'And there's no doubt about the identification this time. True, this new body looks like Faun Moran and you say the fingerprints agree.'

'Indeed, and the father came and identified his daughter and her dental records match. I think there is little doubt.'

'Were her dental records not checked after the car accident?'

'As I told you, the car had rolled several times, the head was badly damaged, and then the fire seems to have finished the job. From what I understand the face was seriously damaged and disfigured and then, of course, burned beyond recognition.'

'Convenient,' Henry commented. 'And who led the first investigation? I'm assuming it was treated as an accident and not as foul play.'

'Evidence was gathered, but you are right. No foul play was suspected. It seemed a simple matter of the young man having too much to drink and driving too fast and misjudging a bend. The coroner decreed that this was an accidental death, the family chose not to bring a civil suit and the case was closed. As to who led the investigation, such as it was . . .' For the first time he seemed hesitant and Henry looked keenly at him. 'Well, that would be a Detective Inspector Harold Shelton. Late of the Yard, now serving in the Cheshire Constabulary. Given the importance of the victims, the local police asked for assistance and he was sent up there. He has been given instructions to make himself available to us and has been called to Scotland Yard to facilitate matters.'

'Well, that is going to be a world of joy,' Henry commented.

'Indeed it is,' Mickey agreed.

'Vic, are you some kind of idiot? You were supposed to get rid of her, not make an exhibition of the bitch.'

'I left her where she would be seen, and found, and taken home. I thought you would want her father to—'

'Get back here now. Never mind about all of that and why didn't you call me before? I had to find out about all this through the newspapers.'

Vic hesitated. It had taken him a day or so to decide whether he wanted to make contact at all, but he knew he could delay no longer.

He took a deep breath and gripped the telephone receiver hard enough that his knuckles whitened. 'No,' he said. 'After my last job for you, I might not be coming back. We both know what we said.'

'No one walks out on me; she found that out.'

'Perhaps I'm walking now; how do you feel about that?'

'I'll hunt you down, you know that. No one walks out on me. You are no exception.'

He replaced the phone receiver carefully down in the cradle and stood for a moment catching his breath, steadying himself. His body was shaking, with excitement, with fear? With adrenaline, certainly. But he walked away with a strange lightness in his step and his spirit. What was the worst his boss could do? Kill him? He was glad he had done what he had done, made sure the girl was found. The rest of it would play out in its own way and it would have consequences, he knew that. But sometimes risks had to be taken. Risk was what made life enjoyable. And the game they played brought risk and reward aplenty.

TWO

D I Harold Shelton. Henry thought about him as he shaved the following morning. Shelton was a small, shrew-like man with a taste in loud jackets and fancy hats. Last time Henry had seen him he had worn a black fedora decorated with a leather band through which several fishing flies were pinned. He was a busy seeming man, always on the move – a trait which matched his shrew-like appearance, Henry thought. Though his busyness, in Henry's opinion, did not always yield valid results. He was also a man so confident in his own opinion that he never asked for a second or questioned that first opinion, even should the evidence show otherwise.

Was that being unfair? Henry paused with the straight razor close to his cheek and thought about it. Decided that it wasn't. This obstinacy had seen the DI demoted to DS and then threatened with further demotion. He had narrowly avoided this by leaving Scotland Yard and finding a post across the country in Cheshire, a constabulary that was building up its stock of inspectors and detectives, and perhaps with an interview board that Henry found himself assuming must have been more impressed by the fact that the man had worked at Scotland Yard than by his sudden loss of standing.

Henry and Mickey had had several run-ins with the man before he left. None of them had been major but they left a bad taste in the mouth because this man was so unwilling to even listen to a second opinion, particularly from an officer of lesser rank. On two occasions, when Mickey had cause to work with him, he had disregarded the sergeant's crime scene analysis to such an extent that evidence had been ignored that might have proved someone innocent. Mickey had gone over Shelton's head to report this, and that action had led to a disciplinary hearing and had been part of the evidence that had led to his demotion. That Henry had backed Mickey's affirmation and spoken up for his sergeant meant that neither could be viewed favourably by Harold Shelton, even though he had now regained his original rank.

Henry took a moment to acknowledge the satisfaction that he, now DCI, outranked the man and another moment, this time of guilt and disappointment, that Mickey did not. His sergeant undoubtedly had the ability but seemed unwilling to apply for the promotion that he knew, for various reasons, he would not get despite his skills. The fact that Mickey's actions over Shelton had caused him to be labelled a trouble-maker had certainly not helped his cause. Mickey might have been morally right in his actions, but he had acted against a senior officer, a senior officer who had come from a class far above that of the sergeant's, and Henry knew what impact that had on Mickey's prospects.

He finished shaving and dashed cold water on his face, then patted it dry. Mickey, of course, was right. It was time for Henry to get himself back in the saddle. He couldn't hide out at Cynthia's place forever. So in the morning he and Mickey would go to inspect the body, and in the meantime he could study the reports of the vehicle accident that had so injured Malcolm Everson and, presumably, killed the young woman who had been with him.

The familiar emotions – excitement, curiosity, the thrill of the puzzle and, if he was honest, the chase – were awakening with a force he had not reckoned on. Cynthia was right, Henry thought, he was ready to get back to work. But then, Henry was used to his sister being right.

At breakfast Henry discovered that his sergeant had already been on the phone making appointments for the morning. First stop was to interview the two couples and the younger brother who had seen the body being placed on the beach. Then they would speak to the constable and after that the funeral director who had taken the photographs. After that they would go to the mortuary and view the body. The post-mortem had not yet taken place, delayed until the detectives could get there; Mickey had known that his boss would want to see the unfortunate young woman as she had been found.

Later, they would catch the evening train to London and the following morning would speak to Detective Inspector Shelton and talk through his investigation of the car crash.

'I would like to go and see the crash site,' Henry said.

Mickey nodded. 'Near Matlock in Derbyshire,' he said. 'The house party was close by, only five miles from the crash site. I have contacted the owners of the house and they have agreed to speak to us though they think they can tell us little more. There should have been a guest list in with the evidence from the original investigation, but I could find none. I have asked the Belmonts to produce one for us. I think it would be useful to speak with those who claimed to have seen Faun get into the car.'

Henry nodded approval. 'Presumably they knew the girl well enough to recognize her,' he said. 'The witness statements give no sense of how close they were, or how certain. They are slight and scant from what I've seen so far. Two girls who saw her from the window, a young man smoking on the driveway when the car was driven away and who claims to have seen Everson get into the car with a girl that he assumed was Faun. It was a summer afternoon so they would have been clearly visible. One of the girls mentions that Faun was dressed in red and she saw a girl in a red dress get into the car, but how many girls with red dresses would have been at the party? The other seemed more insistent that it was Faun Moran but . . .'

'Indeed,' Mickey agreed.

'I found no photographs of the crash site.'

'Some were taken, but where they are now I have no idea,' Mickey admitted.

Henry frowned, sometimes things were mislaid, but it was unusual. The record-keeping at the Yard was generally meticulous. He drained his coffee cup and set it down. 'We have two big questions to answer, Mickey. Two major questions at least. Who was the young woman in the car and where has Faun Moran been all this time?'

'Not to mention who was the man on the beach and how she died.'

'If we discover where she has been then I believe we will

discover the rest,' Henry told him. 'If the girl in the car was a guest at the party then someone would have reported her missing by now. Or so I would have thought.'

'No one was reported missing,' Mickey confirmed. 'Though when I was speaking to the Belmonts earlier they told me that not all of the guests were invited – some had come along with others and there were also musicians and professional dancers and hired help. They warned me that their list might be very incomplete.'

'And what was this party in aid of?' Henry asked.

'Actually I believe it was some kind of benefit for musicians and actors who have fallen on hard times. The Belmonts are very keen on that kind of thing apparently. The invited guests had paid a fair amount to attend, apparently, and if they brought additional people with them they were expected to contribute further, but there is no telling who did or how much. I'm told Mrs Belmont sees herself as a patron of the arts and I get the impression Mr Belmont prefers to just let her get on with it. It was the younger Belmonts who were actually giving the party, two daughters and a son. One daughter will be there when we go up; the other siblings are away from home.'

Henry nodded, satisfied. Mickey had laid the groundwork in his usual efficient manner. So, he thought, the young woman in the car could possibly have been a guest, more likely someone who had come with a guest, or someone who was performing. Why had no one missed her? Or if they had and reported her absence, had they not known that she had been at the party? Or was she someone who was expected to be out of touch, so her lack of contact had not been noticed. Mickey's wife, Belle, was an actress and until recently had continued to tour. She had written home several times a week and Mickey had written to her, sending the letters to post offices or boarding houses where Belle could collect them. But a younger, unmarried, untethered woman might not be so assiduous.

'So we have two dead young women,' Mickey said quietly. 'One at least can be returned to her family, even if they have no idea where she has been all this time. The other is missing and no doubt being missed and we do not even have her name.'

Henry nodded soberly, knowing that although they would deal fairly with both victims, Mickey's sympathies perhaps lay more with this unknown girl and her unknown family who did not know where their daughter was and to whom she had not yet been returned.

Vic

He remembered how she had looked, sitting in the back seat of the car, Malcolm Everson's head resting on her lap. The young man was completely out of it, his long-limbed body crammed on to the seat of the car, and she had taken hold of him and pulled him close, and Vic felt that it was more for her own comfort than from any that she could offer to her friend.

She looked terrified, tearful, clearly a woman out of her depth, and he had felt sorry for her. But what could he do? She had dug the hole that she was now in and he could not help to pull her out, even if he wanted to. She was committed now. He had promised to help her, knowing how unhappy she was at home, knowing how much she wanted to escape, and though this was perhaps an unconventional means of exit, Vic could think of no other as certain or as guaranteed to upset those she was running from.

Looking at her, glancing at her reflection in the rear-view mirror, seeing her at this strange mirror distance, he thought that she was someone who would always be running from something because she didn't have a single idea in that pretty head regarding what she actually wanted to do with her life. She was, however, he had thought, beginning to realize that this was not it.

THREE

Mr Colin Chambers and his wife lived only a few minutes' walk from Cynthia's. Their neighbours, the Fullers, who had also been on the promenade, resided only two doors away from them. The younger brother-in-law, Brian Housman, lived elsewhere, and in any case was at work. He had left word that he would be happy to talk to the detectives should they need him. He could tell them little, his sister said; she had sent him off in pursuit of a constable within moments of seeing the man and realizing what he was carrying. 'The arms and legs were hanging down and it was obviously a woman.'

The Fullers had joined the Chambers this morning and both men were impatient to get off to their jobs of work, having taken time off to give interviews to the police officers. They gave a brief account of having walked along the promenade with their wives and children, seeing the man on the beach and noting how strangely he was looking at them. He had been coming along the beach from the opposite direction and had glanced their way several times. When he drew level he had paused, turned, looked directly at them and then placed the body on the sand before walking away. Mickey went over their story several times but it was clear that the men had discussed it between themselves and had settled on this particular set of memories. There would be nothing more to gain. Henry let them go and they set off, grateful that they would have missed only an hour of the morning in their respective offices.

The women seemed to settle themselves when their menfolk had gone. Henry had often noticed that women left alone had more to say and that women often noticed things that men did not. He could hear children playing, running down the hall and laughing. Mrs Chambers glanced towards the door and

Mrs Fuller smiled. 'Ellen will take care of them,' she reassured her friend, and although it was not her house she leaned forward and poured everyone more tea. The two women were clearly very comfortable with one another, Henry thought. Ellen was presumably a maidservant.

'Tell me everything you saw, everything you thought,' he said. Mickey sat poised, pen in hand, watching both women carefully and thoughtfully.

'Well,' Mrs Chambers said, 'we were walking slowly. Our oldest is only five and we knew we would eventually have to carry the two little ones, but they had been so confined to the house with the bad weather we felt it was better for them to have a walk. So we left early, took a slow and easy stroll along the promenade and we chatted, you know, as friends do, and then I saw the man. He was walking along the beach, coming from the opposite direction, and the first thing I noticed was how big he was, how tall. So I said to Frida, Mrs Fuller, look at that man, isn't he big? And then I wondered what it was he was carrying. It looked as though he was carrying something quite substantial, but he was just striding along as though whatever it was weighed nothing.'

'And then I looked too,' Mrs Fuller said. 'And I noticed that he seemed to be glancing in our direction and I said as much to Mrs Chambers, to Carol.'

'And I agreed. He did seem to be glancing over at us, so we mentioned it to our husbands. They were walking just behind us. Karl was walking with them, that's the five-year-old, and we had the two little ones. I was carrying little Flo, and Frida had hold of Elsie's hand. She does like to walk, that one. Well, of course, our husbands were a little concerned, and they agreed with us that this man was definitely looking in our direction.'

Frida picked up the story once more. 'He was walking much faster than we were and he soon drew level with us. He was down on the firm sand just above the waves and you could see his footprints quite clearly. He had big feet; he was a big man.'

'And when he got level with us he stopped dead. And then he turned around to face us and we could see what it was he was carrying.' Mrs Chambers' hands fluttered lightly as though suddenly disturbed by the memory.

'We could all see that it was a girl. As he turned one of her shoes fell off. She had long legs hanging down from one of his arms and her arms were hanging down from the other. She was draped over his arms, I suppose you would say with her head falling back and her scarf trailing and almost touching the floor.'

'Well, you can imagine how shocked we were. My first instinct was to shout at him, then I thought he'd never hear me in this wind, and Brian realized at once what was happening, and he said he would run and find the constable – there's always one patrolling close to the promenade at that time of the morning. In fact, we had said good morning to him as we walked down. So Brian ran off to find a constable and we stood and watched. I mean, what else could we do?'

'We wondered if she was ill,' Mrs Fuller said. 'But she looked . . . Dead. Utterly limp, just lying in his arms like that. When Brian ran off the man bent down and put the body on the sand. He didn't drop her or anything – he bent down very slowly and laid her out by his feet, and then he turned around and walked away back the way he'd come. He didn't run, he didn't even hurry, just turned and walked away.' She shuddered.

'You know,' Mrs Chambers said, 'I think that was the most frightening thing of all. He wanted us to see him, he wanted us to see what he had, but he wasn't in the least bit frightened or concerned. It was as though he knew we couldn't do anything.'

She glanced at Mrs Fuller, who nodded in agreement. 'And then Brian came back with the constable and we stood on the promenade and waited with the children while Brian, the constable and my husband went on to the beach. And they found the girl lying there, just as he had left her, but she was getting wet – the waves were lapping at her. I felt sorry for the poor constable – I think he wanted to chase after the man but he knew he had to do something for the poor dead girl. So he left Colin and Brian standing there and then he ran off to get another constable, and then a vehicle arrived from the undertaker and she was taken away.'

'It all happened quite quickly,' Mrs Fuller said. 'Of course we went home then because we knew that the police would want to talk to us, so we went to church for the evening service. And anyway the children were getting cold, because they had been standing for quite some time. It was also very disturbing.'

'You noticed this man was very big,' Mickey said. 'Taller than the inspector, would you say?'

Henry obligingly stood up. He was a little over six feet tall. Both women nodded.

'Definitely taller, I would say,' Mrs Chambers told them. 'Much broader too. He was a big man, someone who would have stood out as a big man even in a crowd. You would notice him. He had dark hair but he was a little too far away for us to see any more detail than that.'

'But there was something deliberate about the way he moved,' Mrs Fuller added. 'As we told you, there was no hurry, he was just walking very steadily away and his strides, as you would expect, were long but he wasn't . . . awkward . . . like some big men are, you know? What I mean is sometimes they're not quite sure where their arms and legs end. This man was confident; he moved like a soldier, if you know what I mean. Like the guards outside the palace. They're all tall but they're not awkward.'

She glanced at her friend and Mrs Chambers nodded again. 'He was very straight, kept his head up. You know how some very tall people stoop, as though they are very conscious of their height. He wasn't like that.'

'And was the man still in sight when the constable arrived?'

The two women glanced at one another, looking a little puzzled, and Mrs Chambers shook her head. 'I don't think he was. I think, Inspector, we were somewhat fixated on the body of that young woman, staring at her and not quite able to believe what we were seeing. When I looked again in the direction that the man had gone I could not see him. I watched him for a moment or two as he walked away but then I think I must have looked back at the girl and when I looked for him again he was gone.'

'There are steps not far along the promenade,' Mrs Fuller

added. 'We think it's likely he went up the steps and disappeared into the side streets. But he's a big man – surely someone would have seen him.'

'Interesting,' Henry said as they walked back down the street. 'So now we go and have a chat with the constable who was summoned to the scene, though I doubt he will be able to add much. There might have been sightings of such a large individual unless he got into a car and drove away, of course.'

'That seems most likely,' Mickey agreed. 'He must have transported the body somehow but why on earth decide to leave her on a beach? If he wanted her found he could have, I don't know, propped her up in a church porch or something.'

Henry grunted agreement, a little struck by the incongruity of the image his sergeant had produced. 'And the women were right – he would have stood out in a crowd so the chances are someone else spotted him that morning but did not realize they were seeing anything significant.'

'True, but not many people were around, and most that were I imagine had their heads down and were charging into the wind, paying very little attention to elsewhere.'

'But if he was a big and solid man, he would have attracted notice. What mitigates against that is the likelihood that he was driving a car and would have waited until the street was empty before he removed the body. But there's a good chance he parked on or close to the promenade and close to the steps leading down to the beach, so that narrows the field a little.'

They had arrived at the police station and asked for the constable. They were told that he was waiting for them and were directed through to the back office. Constable Jones was attending to some paperwork but leaped to his feet as soon as the senior officers entered. Henry waved him back down and Mickey secured two more chairs. Both declined the offer of tea; they had drunk enough tea that morning.

'We've just come from speaking with the Chambers and Fullers,' Henry told him. 'They've given a good account of what took place, but I would welcome your impressions. Could you still see the man when you arrived or had he disappeared from view?'

Constable Jones bristled slightly. 'Had I been able to see him then I would have left Mr Chambers with the body and got the boy to run back for another constable while I gave chase. I looked towards the steps, as that was most likely where he had left the beach, and I thought I heard a car engine, but there was no sign of the man by the time I arrived at where the body lay. So I took a good look at the young lady and then I went to summon a second constable and the undertaker. It was clear there was nothing I could do for her and that there was no sense in calling the doctor. Under normal circumstances I would of course have summoned the police surgeon to the beach, but we had to move the body immediately, to get it out of the waves, and it was clear from the outset that she was thoroughly dead. From the way her head lolled I guessed that her neck had been broken.'

Henry nodded; he had probably taken the best course of action in the circumstances, though it was a pity the body could not have been examined in situ.

'And so you had the body taken to the undertakers—'

'And the police surgeon arrived about the same time as we did. I had him summoned there. He confirmed life was extinct and wrote the certificate. He agreed with me that the poor woman had probably had her neck broken.'

'That her neck *was* broken,' Mickey put in gently. 'We have no evidence as yet that someone did that to her, only that it happened somehow.'

Constable Jones looked mildly offended. 'And then I went back to write my report. But first I went up the steps and I asked anyone who might have been around, knocked on a few doors, asked if anyone remembered the man or if a car had been parked there.'

'And had anyone seen anything?'

'One, Mrs Summers, thought she saw a car parked close to the steps. She said it was blue but that's all she knew. She had taken no notice of it, dismissed it as nothing unordinary. I haven't found no one else that saw anything so far. But I will try again.'

Henry nodded approval and then glanced over at his sergeant.

'Apart from the broken neck, did you notice anything unusual about the body?' Mickey asked.

Henry was sure that Constable Jones would already have given a great deal of thought to the matter; however, Jones was enjoying his moment and he now leant back in his chair, tapping his pen thoughtfully on the arm. 'I noticed that she looked to be expensively dressed. The beadwork on that dress cost a pretty penny, I can tell you that. She wore no jewellery apart from a little clip in her hair and I think that was to hold her headband in place. I said to the undertaker, Mr Jamieson, that I would have expected her to have another one on the other side. These things usually come in pairs in my experience, like dress clips do, but there was just the one, shaped like a little leaf. And then there was her bag, of course, tied to her wrist with a bit of twine. I wondered at the time why whoever had done that didn't just use her scarf. I wondered if it was because they did not want to look at her neck, even though the scarf did not hide the fact that it was broken.'

Interesting, Henry thought.

'And one shoe was missing, but was only a little further along the shoreline, I believe?'

'Yes, one of the ladies said she saw it fall on to the shingle. That beach is mostly shingle, as you know, but here and there is a line of sand exposed and this chap, whoever he was, he had left his footprints in the sand. But they were already filling with water, so of no help to the investigation. And the shoe was in danger of being washed away. I had to fish it out of the waves.' He frowned, and then said, 'And that was the other funny thing I noticed. Pretty shoes they were, black patent, but Chief Inspector, Sergeant Hitchens, I do not believe those shoes to be hers.'

'And why is that?' Mickey asked.

'Because she had tiny feet, sir. She was a slight little lady, as you'll see when you view the body, and the shoe had fallen from her foot because the shoe was too big. I could have slipped a finger between her foot and the heel of the one she still wore. Whoever put those shoes on her feet made a mistake. She would not have put them on herself for they were definitely not her own.'

Henry raised an eyebrow. That also was very interesting. The constable had little more to say after that and so they took their leave.

'With each detail the mystery deepens,' Mickey commented. 'So was the dress hers, I wonder, and is our constable right about the hair clips? Is it significant that she wore no other jewellery? Had that been taken from the body, stolen perhaps after death? Though from what I've seen of the photographs, the bag itself was well made and of value.'

'We should ask Cynthia about the hair clips,' Henry said. 'Though I do know that Cynthia has hair clips to hold such bands in place, or simply to fasten her hair. From what I remember they are usually in pairs. They are also usually paste; they sparkle well but have little value.'

The premises of the undertaker who had first taken charge of the body was back along the promenade, in the opposite direction. Mr Jamieson was waiting for them in his office. He was a tall, thin, grey man: grey hair, grey eyes and pallid skin. He looked, Henry thought, like an ideal fit for his profession. His liveliness of manner belied this. Although his face at rest was lugubrious, once he began to speak and smile there was a brightness in his eye and a flush to his cheek. It was, Henry thought, as though a corpse had suddenly been suffused with blood. Mickey produced the photographs that Mr Jamieson had taken and laid them out on the table.

'We are grateful you had the presence of mind to do this,' Mickey told him, 'and we were wondering if you had any other impressions you might add to the images you captured.'

Mr Jamieson steepled his fingers and surveyed his work with a look of great satisfaction. 'I have been a keen photographer for most of my life,' he said. 'Landscape and portraits mostly, but we keep a camera here so that we can record the work we do for our poor unfortunate clients. Sometimes after a long illness they arrive looking, well, less than their best, and if the funeral is to have an open casket then it does not seem right that their poor relatives and friends should remember them disfigured. I record what remedial work we do as an aide memoir.'

'And an advertisement,' Henry suggested.

'We are very proud of the work we do here.'

Henry murmured uneasily that he was sure they were. He remembered viewing his mother's corpse just before her funeral and thinking that the woman in the coffin looked nothing like her. Hollow-cheeked and sunken-eyed, she was not as he wanted to remember her. Their father had burnt every picture, or so he thought, in a final act of cruelty. Cynthia, of course, had managed to rescue three. Later their father had discovered one and beaten Henry's sister with great viciousness, but the two remaining photographs had stayed hidden, Henry keeping one and his sister the other. The memory he had of his mother was therefore from a time when she was young and beautiful and happy. He doubted any undertaker could have done anything to have made his mother look more acceptable or more like her. He realized that his mind had wandered and that Mickey was asking another question.

'Did you look at the contents of her bag?'

'No, oh no. The constable suggested, and I agreed, that we should not disturb anything. I photographed what I could because I thought it would be important, but we disturbed nothing.'

'And the police surgeon – he simply confirmed death?'

'Yes, he was here within minutes. There was nothing else he could do. He confirmed that the young woman was dead and wrote the certificate, noting the time of his visit and his statement that life was extinguished. The body was still loose and flexible, there was no rigor mortis, and I very much doubt that it had occurred and then passed. My guess would be that the poor unfortunate was just recently dead. I suggested that the doctor take a temperature but he said that she had been in the water so there was little point.'

'It might well have been useful,' Henry agreed. 'From what we understand the girl had not been in the water for very long.'

Mr Jamieson nodded solemnly in agreement, as if decrying the professional inadequacies of the police surgeon. 'The knot is strange,' he said, pointing to the photograph where he had taken a close-up image of the knotted twine that tied the girl's evening bag to her wrist. 'I cannot identify it but it looks elaborate. Not the way someone might simply knot a cord to tie up a parcel, or a joint of meat.'

Henry looked closely and was inclined to agree. He saw

Mickey make a note of this. So far, Henry thought, they had a lot of odd little details to examine, any one of which might give them the lead they required to find who had left the body on the beach and the identity of the large man.

The undertaker had little more to add. He mentioned that a local newspaper had been in touch and asked him for a statement, which he had made. He told them also that a national newspaper had telephoned looking for his observations and asking about the photographs that it seemed they knew he had taken. It was obvious that he was wondering if he might benefit from this and Henry gave him a look that silenced and froze the man.

Mickey gathered up the photographs, put them back in the murder bag and they walked back slowly to Cynthia's house. The appointment for the post-mortem was set for that afternoon so they might as well return to Cynthia's for lunch, and for Mickey to collect his belongings and Henry to pack a case; that way they could go straight to London from the mortuary.

'This is an odd one,' Henry said. 'It is nonsensical. It is as though someone deliberately set out to pile mystery on mystery.'

'But we will get to the bottom of it,' Mickey said confidently.

Henry glanced at his sergeant. Mickey looked content, happy even, now that the status quo had been restored and he was carrying the murder bag for Detective Chief Inspector Henry Johnstone. Henry smiled. The truth was that he was beginning to feel tired and there was still a lot more day and a lot more business to attend to before he could rest. He was not yet fully restored and his arm and shoulder ached abominably. He stuffed a hand into his pocket so that his arm did not hang so heavily and the pain in his shoulder was relieved a little. But that apart, that and the tiredness, he did feel better. Better for being busy and useful and in the company of his friend, Henry thought.

Vic

The first time he saw her, Vic had been smitten. Then he had seen that look in his employer's eyes and had known this girl meant trouble. Trouble far greater than Vic knew how to deal with. However Vic might feel, his boss had chosen this one and Vic had better stand aside. Vainly, he had tried to distract Ben, but once he had a notion in his head there was very little anyone could do to pull him back. The only thing Vic could do under those circumstances was to go along with what he wanted. Ben was a little crazy in the head, had been ever since he'd come home, ever since Vic had brought him back from the front in 1917. Ben's father had known this only too well and that was why he had employed Vic to be his shadow, to tidy up after him, and while the old man had been alive this had worked. Most of the time. Since Mr Caxton passed away there had been a change. Ben had no one but Vic to say no to him now and Vic was, in Ben's eyes, just his employee. Vic no longer had Mr Caxton's authority to rely on. Ben saw Vic as his to order about and his to control. Except that Ben didn't know anything about control. Not in any real sense, especially not when it came to himself. And besides, Vic didn't usually want to be the voice of restraint. The truth was he had initially enjoyed the game just as much as Ben ever did, and though the glamour of it had worn a little thin of late it was still hard to resist.

It was ironically this little touch of craziness that had drawn others to him. A kind of charisma, Vic thought. Or old-fashioned glamour. It was what had brought him admiration, envy, promotion back in the day and which, after he had been wounded and sent back home, had a kind of ruthlessness added to it, fed by anger. No, Vic thought, fed by rage at what Ben saw as the injustice of it all.

Vic watched him that night, watched Ben watching this girl, this Faun Moran. Good family, money, beauty, though she was younger than the women Ben was usually attracted to. She was possessed of the same kind of wild free-spiritedness Ben would recognize because he had shared it once upon a time. That old combination of glorious exhilaration and a little craziness had transmuted to become a twisted thing.

Vic had watched as Ben crossed the room to where the girl was dancing, Cuban-heeled red shoes swivelling on the tabletop, beaded dress twisting and swirling around the slender

*body, the contra rotation reminding Vic for a moment of a dog
that had just emerged from water and was shaking itself dry.*

*The music ended with a flourish and the girl took a bow,
laughing, her pretty face flushed and lightly sheened with
sweat. She looked for a hand to help her down and Ben was
there, palm outstretched. Vic had held his breath. Ben's gloves
hid the scarring on his hands but not on his face. Would she
recoil? Would she fail the test?*

*But the girl called Faun Moran just took the outstretched
hand, stepped down upon a chair, then on to the floor. She
took her hand back and smiled happily at him and then turned
and was swept up into the dancing crowd as the band struck
again. Ben watched her go and Vic watched Ben and his heart
flipped a little as he saw the look in his employer's eyes. This,
he had known, would not end well. Not for the girl, anyway.*

FOUR

The mortuary was at the Royal Victoria Hospital and by two o'clock that Wednesday afternoon they were surveying the body. Mickey was aware that his boss was feeling the strain and hoped that Henry would be able to sleep on the train as they headed towards London. He knew that Henry did not find post-mortems easy and had suggested that they remain only for the preliminary examination, collect the poor young woman's possessions and have the rest of the report sent to them. There was in truth little reason to delay.

Mickey was slightly annoyed to find that the girl had already been undressed and her clothes folded neatly and left on a bench at the side of the white tiled room. He wanted to know if the clothes had fitted her as badly as the shoes. The shoes stood beside the dress and he picked one up, crossed to the body and tried it on the foot.

'Our constable was right,' he commented. 'The shoes are too big.'

Henry had unfolded the dress and was examining it carefully. 'It's heavy,' he said, weighing the dress in his hands. 'The beading is exquisitely done, the label is French. It is difficult to tell if the size is hers,' he added, looking pointedly at the mortuary assistant.

Mickey set the shoe down beside its fellow. 'Was she wearing stockings?'

The mortuary assistant had the grace to look shamefaced and shook his head. 'No, sir, just what you see there. No stockings.' He rallied a little and then said, 'And no mark of garters on the legs, so they had not been removed. Seems to me like the young lady had just not put them on.'

Mickey nodded briefly and examined the underclothing more carefully. Silk, he thought, and again of excellent quality. It was cut in that way that made things stretch – what did Belle call it? On the bias, that was it, which he knew made it more

expensive. Belle had described some of Cynthia's clothes that
way and how clever it was and how extravagant in terms of
fabric. 'But the underclothes are too big too,' he said. 'That
might not be noticed with the dress because the beads would
make it hang more closely to the body, but the underclothes
. . . it seems to me they are made for a plumper and taller
woman.' He could see from Henry's expression that his boss
agreed.

'But if you want to dump a body, why dress it so extra-
vagantly?' Henry asked. 'It seems so unnecessary. So . . .'

Mickey watched as his boss searched for the word. 'Showy,'
Mickey said simply. 'Well, whoever it does belong to, I can't
see them being too pleased when they found out it was missing.
And what woman would agree to having a costume like this
used to dress a corpse?'

'It is an interesting question.'

Mickey folded the clothes and placed them in a brown
paper bag, then put that in the murder bag. They turned their
attention to the evening purse that had been tied to Faun
Moran's wrist. The contents were unexpected. A party invitation from six months before with Miss Moran's name on it.
It was for the Belmonts' party, he noted, the one she had
supposedly left in Everson's car and been driven to her death.
A business card with her father's office address. A small
comb, ivory, engraved with flowers. A silver powder compact
and a lipstick.

'An odd assortment of objects,' Mickey said. 'It suggests
she attended the party and has not touched or at least not
emptied this bag since.'

The bag itself was of a fine quality, the chainmail fluid and
delicate and undoubtedly silver. The frame of the bag was
enamelled with little butterflies. The chain was also unusual,
in that it looked like a braid or a twist, and when he crossed
to the body and examined the wrist Mickey could see where
it had been twisted around and left marks in the flesh. The
original intention had probably been that this should be enough
to hold the bag in place and then whoever had done it had
second thoughts and tied it more firmly with twine.

He came over to where Henry was examining the string

with its elaborate knot. 'At least this has not been untied,' he said. 'The knot is still intact.'

'I couldn't undo it, sir,' the mortuary assistant said. 'So I'm sorry, sir, but I had to cut the string.'

'Well, thank heavens for small mercies,' Henry muttered.

The mortuary assistant knew he was in the doghouse, Mickey thought, but really hadn't got a clue why. The surgeon who was carrying out the post-mortem arrived at that point, and after introductions he began his preliminary examination and Mickey announced their intention to leave before the post-mortem was complete. The surgeon seemed unconcerned at that.

'Well, it's pretty obvious to me that the cause of death is a broken neck,' he said.

'But did someone break her neck, or was it accidental? That's the question,' Mickey told him.

'And it may well be one I cannot answer. The neck is broken. I will examine the throat for bruising, but unless there was very rough handling it's unlikely I can say definitively one way or another.'

And with that, Mickey thought, they would have to be satisfied.

A little later, on the way to the train station, Henry said, 'Why was she not dressed in her own clothes?'

'That is a leading question,' Mickey agreed. 'Though perhaps we should also ask why she was naked when she died, as presumably she must have been if someone had to fully redress her.'

'True,' Henry agreed.

'I suppose if the clothes were larger, they would have been easier to put on. Women's garments are something of a mystery to most men. You watch a woman get dressed and she wriggles her way into things. A deadweight is much harder to dress, that's for certain.'

'So do we think the man dressed her?'

'That we can't know. But she certainly didn't dress herself.'

FIVE

I t was the first time that Henry had stayed overnight in his London flat since he had been injured. He had returned to his home only once to collect things he needed, but otherwise the flat had been cleaned once a week by a woman his sister had engaged for that purpose and who posted his mail on to him, also weekly. He supposed now he ought to prepare for moving back.

He pushed the door open, shifting letters out of the way with his foot and then bending to pick them up. He flicked through them as he walked through to his living room, switched on the electric fire and then went through to the kitchen to turn on the gas rings. The flat was chill and cold and felt unloved, and for that he was sorry. With his coat still on he sat down in what had always been his favourite chair and stared out of the window with its view of the river.

His mail turned out to be a mix of bills and circulars. The last time he had returned to the flat had been a few days before Christmas. He had been in pretty rough shape at the time. The manservant his sister had sent with him to drive and to help him up the stairs had been terribly concerned that he might pass out, Henry remembered. It had been mortifying, directing someone else to pack his clothes and sort out the possessions he wanted to take back to Cynthia's, and he had been profoundly relieved when the task had been finished and he had been driven home. And Cynthia's place had been home, he realized. He had ceased to think about these few rooms as somewhere he belonged. So how did he feel about that now? Henry still wasn't sure. He had brought a couple of newspapers on the way home. Mickey had been enthused by news of Australian cricketer Donald Bradman. Apparently his 452 not out was a record for his innings in a match against

Queensland. Henry was not especially interested in cricket, but he noted the daily score of murder and violence in his home city and read with some cynicism that the second Hague conference on German reparations was still sitting. What good would it do to bleed a country white, Henry wondered, when there was already social unrest and overwhelming poverty for so many? If anything was guaranteed to sacrifice the peace then surely this was it.

He set the paper aside, not wanting to read any further stale or dispiriting news. The day had tired him out and Henry must have drifted into sleep. He woke with a start to realize that it was now fully dark outside, and his watch told him that it was past ten. Wearily, he dragged himself off to bed aware that the sheets felt damp. Then he got up again, going through to the kitchen to switch off the gas rings and then the living room fire. The rooms at least felt warmer now and he was too exhausted to worry too much about damp sheets.

That night he dreamt about the cellar. It was the first time in weeks that it had invaded his mind in sleep. That dank, cold, dark place where Melissa had been imprisoned and where he had nearly lost his life when he had gone to rescue her. The cold seeped into his bones. He tossed restlessly and finally woke with a start and the dreadful sense that someone else was in the room with him.

Henry held his breath and sat up slowly, looking around, but there was nowhere to hide in the small bedroom. He padded through to the living room and kitchen, examined the bathroom, but there was no sign of anybody or of anyone having been there and the bolts were still fast on the front door. He had been dreaming, Henry realized. The damp of the sheets had reminded him of the damp cellar. The memory of being attacked from behind had no doubt infiltrated his over-exhausted mind. That was all there was to it. But he still felt shaken.

Looking at his watch, he saw it was four a.m. He made himself some tea, remembering belatedly that there was no milk and he would have to drink it black. He switched on the electric fire and settled himself in his chair, wrapping a blanket from his bed around his shoulders and his counterpane across his knees. He fell asleep again without drinking his tea and woke only to the sound of Mickey Hitchens knocking on his door just after eight.

Henry was acutely aware of his sergeant's scrutiny when he let him in.

'You should have come back with me,' Mickey told him acerbically. 'We have a spare room and you know Belle would love to have seen you.'

'I have to be on my own at some point, Mickey,' Henry replied. 'I cannot stay forever at Cynthia's, or even with you, not if I am back at work.'

Mickey frowned and settled himself in Henry's chair while his boss got dressed and ready to leave. Today they would be travelling up to Derbyshire, to speak with the Belmonts tomorrow, but before that he had an appointment at New Scotland Yard to discuss the car accident that everyone had believed had killed Faun Moran with DI Harold Shelton, who had come to London for the purpose.

DI Shelton was as weaselly as Henry remembered. And his jacket was as loud. Today he was sporting a windowpane check, blue against a yellowish background, that caused Henry to feel slightly nauseous. The man was clearly nervous, grinning too often and fiddling with paperwork that had been placed on Henry's desk.

It was, Henry thought, strange to be back at his desk.

He had been welcomed enthusiastically by his colleagues, most of whom had kept in touch while he had been away, but Henry had realized that he had actually been quite nervous when he walked back into the Central Office. He had almost expected to find his desk invisible under a pile of someone else's investigation, or even been given to someone else. He expected life to have gone on, of course, but had almost assumed that he himself would have been written out of it. He was relieved to find that this was not the case.

He now regarded DI Shelton with barely hidden distaste. So far, the man had gabbled a lot but relayed little of any use.

'We expected there to be crime scene photographs,' Henry said.

'And indeed there were, there were, indeed. But where they are, I have no idea. You must understand I left very shortly thereafter. I know nothing about this. A road accident, tragic certainly, but that was all.'

'But surely photographs would have been taken to see how the car came off the road, where it ended up? Pictures of the body, and of where the young man had landed when he was thrown clear.'

'And as I said, Chief Inspector, photographs were taken, but where they are I have no idea. I no doubt filed everything in the appropriate places. If the photographs are now gone, that is not my responsibility.'

His tone verged on insolent, Henry thought. Across the desk he could see that Mickey was frowning and looking as impatient as his boss felt. Henry took a deep breath. 'And so, tell me what your observations were. Your accident report is scant on detail.'

Inspector Shelton stared at the report that Henry pushed across the desk to him. 'An accident,' he said. 'It was only because of the personages involved that the Yard was called upon at all. An accident is something the local constabulary could and should have dealt with. But someone realized that the gentleman involved was of some importance, and then it was reported that the young lady involved was also a lady of some substance and so we were called in case there had been foul play. There was none, of course. The young gentleman was drunk. He should not have been driving. He took the bend too fast and the result was a crash and conflagration and the poor unfortunate young woman lost her life. The coroner found that it was accidental, of course, so what more was to be done?'

He had a point, Henry conceded, but he did not feel terribly charitable. Shelton's report was brief, terse and lacking in detail, and the photographs were missing, which was a deep annoyance. 'So, your impressions and observations?'

Shelton sat back in his chair and sighed. He laced fingers across his mustard waistcoat and frowned. 'The young gentleman was unconscious and the young woman was burnt beyond recognition. The car was remarkably intact considering. And now I believe there is a deeper mystery – that the young lady is not the young lady everyone thought had died.'

Henry was staring at him. 'What do you mean the car was remarkably intact?'

'Exactly that. From the state of the young woman's body I would have expected it to have been burned to a crisp, and true, it was badly fire-damaged, but the *rear* of the car, the rear of the car was surprisingly intact. The luggage compartment had burst open on impact and baggage had been scattered in all directions, but the boot of the car itself was merely scorched by the flames. The local constable thought that the car had burst into flames, but then the rolling put it out.'

'And does that seemed likely?' Henry asked coldly.

'But what is the other explanation?' Shelton asked. 'The facts are as stated in my report. The car came off the road, tumbled down the hill, and from the amount of damage done to the undergrowth it probably rolled several times. The farmer who gave evidence certainly considered that to be the case, judging from the sounds he had heard.'

Could you actually judge the number of times something rolled purely on hearing it happen? Henry wondered, but he said nothing.

'And when did the farmer arrive?' Mickey interposed.

'Why, very quickly, I imagine, perhaps five minutes, perhaps ten. I did not walk the distance. Why should I? On hearing the crash the farmer sent his boy to fetch the doctor and the local constable, and the youth set off by bicycle, I believe, and the farmer himself came to the scene, expecting the worst, of course, and finding it. He brought one of his farmhands with him, as you'll see from my report. They found the young man's body halfway down the slope, and at first thought him dead. Then they saw the car, the body in the front passenger seat, as I say, burnt beyond recognition, and evidence of burning, of course, in the car itself.'

'But the fire had gone out. Your report is a little vague.'

Shelton hesitated. He was beginning to see what they were

getting at and not liking the direction things were going in. 'I believe out or as near as made no matter. They were very fortunate the petrol tank had not exploded. There is a stream at the bottom of the hill,' he added as though suddenly relieved to have remembered this. 'I believe the car had landed on its roof – of course it did not have a roof, the car, it was an open-topped vehicle, but anyways it landed on its top in the stream. Yes, that was it.' He poked at his notes, dabbing a finger at a passage. 'I mentioned the stream. I'm sure I mentioned the stream.'

Ostentatiously Henry took up the paper and examined it thoroughly before laying it back on the table. 'No stream is mentioned,' he said.

'Well, if we had photographs, I could point out the location to you; I could indicate where the car landed. We would have evidence of it landing in the stream. Clearly that's what put the fire out.'

'And yet we do not have the photographs,' Henry said.

'No, well, quite, that is my problem. That is *your* problem, should I say. If we had the photographs it would be clear.'

Henry sighed; he doubted that. 'A fire hot enough to have reduced a young woman's body to an unrecognizable mass would have been fierce and not easily extinguished,' he said. 'And the young woman was still in the car.'

'As I have just told you, in the front passenger seat. And there was evidence of burning in the front of the car. No doubt fierce burning, as you say.'

'And yet you say the rear of the car was not completely burned out.'

Frowning now, his hands no longer laced across his belly, Shelton nodded. 'That is the case,' he agreed. 'I am no expert in cases of automobile accidents or of automotive fires. How can I say what might be expected and what might not?'

'And this luggage you mentioned. Where was that?'

'Why, it was scattered around the place. Thrown out no doubt when the car rolled down the slope.'

'And is there a list?'

Shelton shuffled through the notes on the desk. There was
not. 'I made a list,' he insisted. 'A list of items found to be
still in the car and a list of items scattered along the line of
its descent.'

'And where is that list?'

'How the . . .' He bit back on his annoyance. 'I don't
know. Separated from the report at some time, no doubt, as
were the photographs. I can't possibly know what became
of either.'

'But can you at least recall what might have been on it?'

Shelton hesitated, then closed his eyes and thought hard.
The effort was obviously causing him pain, Henry thought.
At last, Shelton said, 'A picnic basket, a leather Gladstone bag
. . . I think that belonged to the young man, as male clothing
was spread about the place. And a small blue suitcase, I believe.
That must have belonged to the girl. Women's clothing had
been strewn along the way, too.'

He opened his eyes and looked satisfied as though expecting
congratulations.

Henry moved restlessly, impatient now, and was relieved
when Mickey took over.

'At least we have the farmer's name, and that of his farmhands, and the attending physician,' he said. 'Perhaps they can
be more forthcoming.'

Shelton bristled, realizing that he was being insulted.
'Sergeant Hitchens, I am your superior officer, and your tone
is verging on the insolent. I have come all this way to be of
assistance to you – the least I can expect is politeness.' He
looked pointedly at Henry as though expecting him to
reprimand his sergeant. Henry would do no such thing.

He glanced at his watch. Unlike Mickey, Henry wore a
wristwatch, another present from Cynthia and much treasured.
'I will arrange for a driver to take you back to the station,'
Henry said. 'I'm sure you're eager to return to your present
constabulary.' Then, because he knew he ought to be polite,
he thanked Shelton for coming and handed him his
overcoat.

'What a bloody mess,' Mickey remarked when Shelton had
gone. 'I don't like the sound of this, Henry. None of this is

right. For a young woman to be burned to death in the car
fire, the fire would burn fiercely and long enough to consume
the body. We have both witnessed death by burning, and it is
a terrible thing. And we have both witnessed vehicles that
have burnt. It is a fate I only just escaped myself in the war.
This does not ring true.'

Henry nodded. The incident that Mickey referred to was
one that was all too fixed in Henry's memory. If he had not
been there that day Mickey might well have not survived.

'I had asked for the post-mortem reports on the young
woman that died in the automobile accident, but it seems none
was carried out. Apparently Mr Moran came and took the
body away, declaring that he would not have his daughter
carved up to no purpose. I believe there were some arguments,
but by the time the inquest had determined that this was indeed
an accident she had already been interred. It is highly irregular,
but then I believe so is Caius Moran and some people, as we
know, are wealthy enough to buy themselves out of any situation they do not like. However, now that we know this girl
is not Faun Moran it's to be hoped that we can have the body
examined and learn something more. But you are right. The
more we dig the more mysteries we uncover. There is nothing
straightforward in this business.' Henry glanced at his watch
again. In less than an hour they too would be taking the train
to Derby. 'I'm hoping the farmer will have more sense than
DI Shelton,' he said. 'And that he will have been more
observant.'

Mickey laughed. 'He can hardly have been less so.'

'True, though to be fair I cannot believe that even Shelton
would have been as careless as the loss of photographs and
other material implies. He is an arrogant man. He was often
wrong in his initial assumptions and we know he was always
unwilling to change direction, even when the evidence was
against him. But his paperwork, though lacking in detail,
was usually well kept. He took pride in that fact, if you
recall.'

'You could be right,' Mickey acknowledged. 'I must admit
that my prejudice colours my recollections of the man, but
no, it does seem odd. For a packet of photographs to be

misplaced, that I could understand, but for other documents to also be missing does seem strange. You think they were removed deliberately?'

Henry shrugged. 'I think it's possible. Though even those details Shelton did recall are strange, and not just regarding the woman's body. That both young Malcolm Everson and the woman who was not Faun Moran had baggage in the car implies that this was more than a simple drive. They were headed somewhere, perhaps to spend the night there. They intended to stop on the way if we judge by the addition of a picnic basket. We had been led to believe, from these very scant witness reports,' he handed the relevant documents to his sergeant, 'that this was a moment of impulse. That Faun Moran wished to go for a drive and so Malcolm Everson leapt into his car, even though it seems he'd been drinking heavily and their friends urged them otherwise. One woman gets into the car, alive and well. Another is found, dead and burnt in such a way that she was identified purely on the evidence of those who saw the couple set off.'

'It was a reasonable enough assumption,' Mickey commented. 'If one young woman sets off on a drive you expect the same young woman to be present when the car stops. For whatever reason it stops.' He paused. 'Perhaps we should be speaking to Mr Maskelyn at St George's Hall. This is worthy of that magician's misdirection.'

'I have a preference for David Devant,' Henry told him, 'but I agree all of this seems terribly theatrical. The staging of the body on the beach simply adds to that sensibility. But if we are to catch that train then we should be moving. Tomorrow we will be able to interview the Belmonts who hosted the party, and also hopefully view the crime scene.'

'Scene of the accident, you mean,' Mickey said, but he was smiling, knowing that Henry was probably right.

'No, I mean the crime scene. The young woman who died . . . the more I look at this the more I am certain her death was not caused by an accident. This is murder, or I am no detective.'

SIX

Faun, October 1929

*T*he first time I went to his house was just after new
year. That was when this whole horrid business really
began. When this vile plan began to form in his head.
I went unannounced and in my own car, and I knew he
might not approve and might not even welcome me, but I
couldn't think of anywhere else to go. Pat was away and I felt
so lonely and so very desperate and he'd always been so kind.
His welcome was everything I had hoped for. He sat me down
and gave me brandy and Vic wrapped a blanket round my
shoulders and suddenly I knew that I could stop crying and
be warm and . . . and even loved.

You can stay tonight, he said, and I felt so happy. I didn't
know what my father would say but I guessed he'd probably
think I'd gone back to London and I knew he wouldn't try
and contact me anyway because he never did when we'd
had a fight. He said he was only trying to do what was best
for me but that was totally bogus. All he wanted to do was
to control my life and to make me behave the way he thought
I should.

I wished my mother was still alive. She would have understood. She would have made it all better. She could even
talk him round. Father loved her more than anything else
in the world. I know that now, and when she died he saw
Pat and I as being so like her that he could barely stand
the sight of us.

So I went to his house and I told him that I loved him and
I poured out my heart and he told me I could stay that evening
and that he'd find a way so I could be with him always.

I believed him. I thought he loved me. I thought he was an
honest man and a kind man but I learnt that he was none of
those things. That he was cruel and sadistic and wanted only

*to control me and every other person in his life. He is worse
than my father ever was.*

Friday 10 January

They had spent the night at the Duke of Wellington and then
caught a local train which stopped at the tiny station serving
the Belmont estate. A chauffeur from the estate was waiting
to take them up to the house, a drive of another two miles.
Henry did not seem disposed to speak and Mickey sat back
enjoying the scenery. He had not been into the Peak District
before, but considered that it was well named and also
outstandingly beautiful. The train had brought them through
a wild landscape – now the car drove them through parkland,
the truly natural giving way to the manufactured naturalistic.
Sheep wandered across the road, others grazed beneath
mature trees and when the house came into view it was not
the gritstone, grey and a little drab, that Mickey had noted
in the villages they had passed through, instead this massive
edifice was faced with limestone, the frontage flat and he
guessed Georgian or at least imitating Georgian. The driver
paused at the front entrance and let them out and then disappeared around the back of the house having murmured that
his employer did not like cars parked on the gravel and that
they only had to send for him when they were ready to leave.

'At least they didn't make us use the servants' entrance,'
Mickey joked.

Henry led the way up the flight of ten steps where the large
front door was already opening and a liveried footman stood
aside and welcomed them in. A middle-aged woman stood in
the wide entrance hall. She was dressed in lilac, a woollen dress
with a heavy cardigan over the top and she had both hands
extended in greeting. 'Come along in. I hope you're not too
cold – there's a good fire burning in the morning room. Would
you like tea or coffee or both? I'll send for both. Jackson, please
take care of it for me.' This last to the footman who bowed and
went on his way.

She introduced herself as Mrs Phyllis Belmont but it was

clear that she was not a woman who stood on ceremony. The morning room was comfortable with overstuffed chairs that were at least, Mickey reckoned, a half century old, strewn with warm woollen rugs and crocheted afghans. This, it seemed, was not a room for guests, more one for family comfort, and he was reminded of Cynthia's house. It seemed that Mrs Belmont knew Henry's sister well because she asked after her immediately, wanting to know how the children were doing, and if Melissa was still enjoying her books. 'I sent her a parcel a little while back. Our brood of course have now well outgrown the children's literature that they once enjoyed so much. Now all they seem to read is magazines. You would not believe what nonsense there is in all of these female journals. I've no time for it myself, but I suppose each generation despises what the new generation loves.' She laughed warmly. 'Melissa sent me such a lovely letter in thanks. She is such a sweet child.'

Mickey glanced in Henry's direction. The one direct way to Henry's heart was to praise Cynthia or Melissa. The boys too – he was very fond of the boys, but he was not so good at talking about cricket and motorcars; that was very much Mickey's domain.

Jackson arrived with a large tray and an accompanying housemaid with another large tray and these were set down on butlers' tables. 'Sergeant Hitchens, I shall appoint you as mother, so if you'll pour the tea or the coffee and I will take care of the cake and the sandwiches.' She smiled at him with a knowing look in her eye which somewhat unsettled Mickey as she continued, 'I have heard so much about you too, both from Melissa and from the boys. Apparently you took them to play cricket on the beach and ended up taking out a boat. I'm told they both got very wet.'

'Indeed I did,' Mickey agreed. 'Cynthia was not amused.' But to be fair she had soon got over her pique and seen the funny side.

For a few minutes they fussed with plates of cake and cups of tea and then Mrs Belmont grew sober. 'This is a bad business,' she said. 'It was a bad business to start with and it can only get worse now that the poor girl has been found dead, all over again. I was dreadfully shocked when the local police came to tell me. What on earth has happened here? I'm not sure how much I can tell you because that weekend we were away from home, but Eliza was here. Our daughter Elizabeth,' she explained.

As though on cue the door opened and a young woman came in. She was, Mickey judged. about nineteen or twenty, long limbed and with shingled hair, but her smile was very much like her mother's. She helped herself to coffee and cake and sat down opposite Mickey, looking at him with interest. He assumed she too knew all about the cricket and the sailing.

'As I said, Eliza was here that weekend. The police questioned her of course, albeit briefly, but anything we can do to help—'

'Not that there's a lot I can tell you,' Elizabeth said. 'I was here, but I didn't see them leave. I heard about it after-wards. The truth is Faun Moran was a flighty sort of girl. She liked the young men, and they liked her, but there was no harm in her. She just liked fun. She would set her cap at somebody or other, some young man, run around like a thing possessed for a while, assuring everybody that she was in love with them, and then a week or two later she'd be on to someone else. She was too, too frustrating at times, and the boys would get upset with her, but I don't think she ever meant harm.'

'And Malcolm Everson, was he her latest interest?' Henry asked.

'Well, that weekend he seemed to be. It wouldn't have lasted, of course, and Mal was the last person to take her seriously – he was well aware of the game. He's a nice boy, it's all been too bad for him. It's all been frightful. He is still not recovered, you know.' There was a warning tone to her voice, something protective, Mickey thought.

'We will be trying to see him, of course,' Mickey said, and saw her scowl.

'Good luck with that,' she said. 'Even his closest, closest friends have been kept at bay. The family have been so protective of him. Of course the poor boy was distraught.'

'He had been drinking,' Mickey reminded her gently. 'I'm sure he feels responsible.'

A moue of discontent joined the scowl on the pretty face. 'He had been drinking, but not to excess. We've talked about this and it's something we don't understand. He had a champagne cocktail when he arrived and perhaps two drinks after that, but Mal was never a big drinker, not like the rest of us.' She glanced towards her mother who was looking at her disapprovingly and then glanced away. 'And that was over several *hours*.'

'I'm told some of his friends tried to dissuade him from driving, that they believed that he had drunk too much.' Henry this time.

'What friends? You tell me who said that. As far as I'm concerned hardly anyone knew they were leaving anyway. I passed them in the hall and they said they were going for a drive. Mal seemed perfectly sober. Our friend Ginny Greaves saw them straight after that and she said they just seemed in high spirits. The local police came and put a few questions to our guests but if you ask me they were just going through the motions. They saw a crashed car, knew that the occupants had been at a house party and just drew their own conclusions. That Scotland Yard detective that was sent here, he didn't even come up to the house.'

Mickey nodded. That did not surprise him. The report on the crash itself had been scant and lacking in detail, it was evident that Shelton had been simply doing the minimum required. 'And would they have had the car brought round the front of the house for them?' Mickey remembered that their chauffeur had suggested the lady of the house did not like cars parked out on the gravel for longer than necessary.

'It would have been easier for them to have gone round to the yard, so I expect that is what they did,' Eliza said. 'Quicker too. We park visitors' cars in the old stable yard; the horses, although we only have three left, live in the new stable block. I expect they went round the back, through the French doors in the dining room, collected the car and went from there.'

'And you are certain that this was the impulse of the moment?' Henry asked her.

'Of course, what else could it have been? Mal said that Faun fancied a drive and so he was going to take her for a quick spin. Those were his exact words; believe me, I have been over and over this many, many times.'

'I'm certain that you have,' Henry said. 'So would you be surprised that they had a picnic basket and two overnight bags in the boot of their car? This would suggest that the young couple planned to stop for a picnic, and then perhaps to spend the night elsewhere.'

'And what do you mean by that, Inspector Johnstone?' Mrs Belmont objected. 'Faun may have had a reputation for being a little wild, and undoubtedly she flirted far too readily, but she was never fast. These were respectable young people.'

'A picnic basket? Overnight bags? But that makes no sense.' Eliza's expression was puzzled now.

'And yet these items were in the boot of the car. They were found at the scene.'

Both women looked completely shocked, though Mickey suspected for quite different reasons. He glanced across at his boss, willing him to shut up for a moment or two, and then said more gently, 'If they had wanted a picnic basket made up, would they have been able to obtain one from the kitchen? Would your cook remember?'

'If she was asked for one, of course,' Mrs Belmont said. 'But most regular visitors to the house would know where the baskets are kept, and believe me, the party was well catered. They could have packed their own basket from the food on the buffet tables without needing to bother any of the servants. It would not be the first time,' she added with a tone of disapproval in her voice that led Mickey to wonder what adventures had previously arisen from such picnics.

'And where are the picnic baskets kept?' Mickey asked. 'Someone might have seen them taking a basket and packing a picnic.'

'There's a little cupboard, between the main hall and the butler's stairs. There are maybe a half-dozen picnic baskets, stirrup cups, even a portable gramophone – they are all kept in there. But as mother says, anyone visiting the house on a regular basis would know that and both Faun and Mal were regular guests.' Eliza looked slightly uneasily at her mother as she said this and Mickey suspected that Mrs Belmont probably did not know how regular and perhaps only had a vague idea of the frequency of her children's parties.

'Do you know what happened to the wreckage of the car and to the other belongings once they were taken from the scene?' Henry asked.

'I have no idea,' Mrs Belmont replied to him.

'I think Mal's family might've arranged for the car to be taken away, but I don't know what happened to it after that. It was a terrible business, Inspector.' Elizabeth turned her face earnestly towards the police officers as though wanting to emphasize just how difficult the whole affair had been.

'And now this,' her mother said. 'What a terrible business, what a terrible, terrible business.'

The chauffeur who had brought them from the station gave them a tour of the stable yard and explained how the dozen cars would have been parked in and around the yard. He remembered that Mr Everson's car had been somewhere close to the middle of the line. 'Mr Everson would have had no problems reversing and manoeuvring to get the car out,' he said. 'He was a very good driver. It was a terrible shock for everyone, what happened.'

'And do you remember anything about that weekend that might help us?' Mickey asked.

The chauffeur shook his head. 'Some of the guests arrived by car, bringing their friends with them, and others I collected from the station. But apart from that I had little to do with the visitors that weekend.'

He drove them to the station shortly after, and Henry sat in the car examining the list of guests, caterers, musicians and dancers who had been present. It was not an exhaustive list, the Belmont women had warned him. Some people had only stayed for a short time; others had been houseguests over the entire weekend.

Mickey sat with his eyes closed visualizing the layout of the house, the drive, the stable yard and the direction that the chauffeur suggested Malcolm Everson might have taken as they left the grounds. 'They would have been invisible to everyone from the house,' he said, 'from the moment they rounded the corner of the building and entered the stable yard. But what puzzles me is why go out through the front entrance when, as Elizabeth Belmont explained to us, they could have gone from the dining room and through the French doors at the rear of the building and then into the stable yard. According to the original report, such as it is, several guests noticed them leaving through the front entrance. However, no one mentioned them carrying luggage, or a picnic basket, which suggests to me that they had loaded the car first and then made a very public exit through the front of the house, wishing to be seen as they left.'

'Telling anybody that they did meet with that Faun Moran had expressed a wish for a quick spin in the car,' Henry agreed.

'So, were they lovers? Was their relationship much closer than anybody suspected? Was there another reason for them leaving the party?'

'Perhaps we will learn more at the scene of the accident,' Henry speculated. 'And then we need to discover where the car was taken to after the event. If the family arranged for it to be taken away then something must have happened to it after that. Was it taken to a scrapyard? Was it stored somewhere?'

Mickey nodded. 'And where did the rumours start that young Everson was drunk, I wonder? He claims to remember nothing, according to the information we have, and he was certainly in no fit state to be tested or examined when they found him at the scene. Elizabeth Belmont is probably correct. The assumption of drunkenness was probably made at the site of the crash, put in the report and not questioned further. The young man had been attending a party, a party that had gone on for a full weekend, ergo he must have been drunk.'

'A simple and logical assumption to have made,' Henry agreed. 'You and I both know that simple and logical assumptions are not always factual. So far Mickey, there is nothing in this case that is simple or logical or factual for that matter. Each time we think we have grasped a fact it slips through our fingers like sand.'

It does indeed, Mickey thought, but at least he and Henry were now examining the facts together, and he found that a great comfort.

SEVEN

Afternoon found them travelling in yet another car, this time with a police driver, Constable Burton, and heading towards the scene of the accident, some five miles from the Belmonts' house. The road rose up into the hills, the land dropping off steeply, through landscape that was heavily wooded, and Henry assumed this was in part to keep the land from slipping. There were somewhat disturbing signs of winter landslides having swept the trees away and, so the driver told them, these had already closed the road on three or four occasions that winter.

He pulled the car on to a narrow grass verge and told them that the crash site was around the next bend, but there was nowhere to park the car any closer. He then led them to where, even six months on, it was obvious that something large had hurtled off the road and down the hillside.

'Did you attend the accident?' Henry asked.

'I did indeed, sir.' Constable Burton nodded. 'We had the devil's own time getting the bodies up and the car was brought up in pieces, so I'm told. I'd gone by that time but Fred Birch from the local garage brought a winch down.' He hesitated and then said, 'It's on the way to Carter's farm. I took the liberty of asking Fred if we could pop in after we've visited the site of the accident. I thought you might find it useful to have a word.'

'That was a good thought,' Henry approved. 'Local knowledge is always useful.' He saw the man relax and caught Mickey's quick smile. Henry knew that he was not always adept at saying the right thing. He knew too that local constabularies were often quite resentful of outsiders from London coming in and taking over. But both Henry and Mickey knew that local knowledge was absolutely essential and were never too proud to acknowledge that fact.

Henry struggled with the scramble down the slope. His left

arm was still lacking strength and the jolting over rough ground hurt his shoulder abominably. He gritted his teeth, clung to the undergrowth as best he could with his right hand and was grateful that he was wearing heavy boots with a good grip on the tread. Mickey and the constable reached the bottom of the hill ahead of him, and Henry arrived to find that the constable was explaining that the car had ended up resting in a small rocky stream that ran the length of the valley floor.

Henry glanced back the way they had come, dreading the climb on their return to the road. He would, he knew, be completely done in by the end of the day. Already the fatigue was so overwhelming that he could have sat on the nearest fallen tree and gone to sleep.

'So what was the position of the car?' Mickey was asking. 'I understood that it was upside down in the stream.'

Constable Burton shook his head. 'No, it had come to rest at a kind of angle, half keeled over so . . .' He picked up a stick and drew in the mud. 'It was not completely tipped, though it was clear it had rolled a few times. The young man had already been taken off to the hospital by the time I arrived. The young lady was still half in the front seat; her ankle seemed to have become wedged and that had held her in place.'

'I'd give my right arm for some photographs,' Mickey said with feeling.

The constable looked puzzled. 'Photographs were taken, sir,' he said.

'And have subsequently been mislaid,' Henry told him. 'Was the car still alight when you saw it?'

Constable Burton shook his head and glanced uncomfortably at Henry. 'I don't want to speak out of turn, sir, especially not against the man – the inspector what came here. I know he is an expert, sir, but none of it seemed right, if you know what I mean.'

'Go on,' Henry told him. 'You can speak freely; your thoughts will not be shared.'

The young constable still looked uncomfortable but he nodded. 'There were three of us came down the slope – the farmer and his son-in-law were already here. This was before the inspector came, it was just after the crash, so I suppose you could say we were seeing it fresh and he was seeing it after.' He looked faintly relieved, Henry thought, as though he had suddenly found an excuse for the senior police officer's lack of judgement.

'It always helps to see a scene when it is fresh,' Mickey confirmed. 'Go on, lad, tell us what you saw.' Henry was aware of Mickey's attention suddenly being fixed on him. 'Perhaps we can sit ourselves comfortably, while you take us through it,' he added, indicating a couple of fallen logs close by.

Gratefully, Henry lowered himself on to one of them and Mickey perched close by. The constable, after a little hesitation, seated himself on the other and then pointed back up the hill. 'We came down where I brought the two of you today. Mr Carter, the farmer, and his son-in-law – they were already down here and the fire was out.'

'Out. Car fires are usually fierce,' Henry said thoughtfully.

'Which was our thinking. But Mr Carter and his son-in-law, they had beat out the flames with branches pulled from the trees nearby. They'd attacked them like we attack grass fires in high summer, we get them up on the high moors. Grass fires aren't so bad, but once it gets in the peat, well that's another matter, but everyone round here knows what they must do when they see a fire. And they had the water from the stream. It's too shallow to be of much direct use, but they were able to soak the car blankets. They grabbed them from the back seat, soaked them and used them to help smother the flames.' He paused and Henry could see that he was looking from himself to Mickey and seeing if they would grasp the importance of his words.

'That was brave,' Mickey said. 'The car had rolled so there would have been fuel spilt everywhere.'

'You could smell it,' the constable confirmed. 'They were scared in case the whole lot went up, but Mr Carter served in the war, he got medals and everything. He's a brave man. He said he could see the young woman was dead, but he was scared in case they couldn't get the young man away, not without help, the slope being so steep, as likely he would have been killed as well. Mr Carter said he couldn't countenance that.'

That sounded like a direct quote, Henry thought.

'And he said the fire weren't that big, not like you'd expect a car fire to be. That's how come they were able to get the blankets. One had been thrown out but one had caught fast and was still in the car.'

Henry nodded his understanding. 'And yet the body was badly burnt?'

The constable hesitated again, and then he said quietly, 'There was a haystack fire two years ago – a vagrant gone to sleep in the stack. You know, maybe, how hot some of them can get. The stack gets damp, it can burst into flame.'

'And is that what happened?'

'Either that, or he dropped a cigarette, whatever way the whole lot went up and the man was dead. He'd probably been drinking, probably didn't wake up. I hope he didn't wake up. But I saw the body, saw how deep the burns went in some places but not so deep in others. When we moved him his skin kind of split and inside, inside you could see that it was still blood and organs and everything, and then in other places he was like charcoal all through, where the burning went deep, even in those parts of the body where you could still see redness inside.' Again, he looked from one to the other as though questioning that they understood, confirming that he wasn't speaking out of turn.

'We have both seen dead bodies, burnt bodies,' Henry confirmed. 'And yes, it is often strange which parts of those bodies are still . . . moist inside and which are burnt crisp. The post-mortem often reveals where the fire began and can be tracked by looking at the pattern of burning. And how did this body look, compared to the one you witnessed before?'

'We all thought, Mr Carter and his son-in-law, and the other constable with me – we all thought it didn't look right. The seat she was sitting on was burned, the carpet on the floor of the car was burned and the inside of the door. The driving seat too – the flame had taken hold there and she was burned all over, all her body, all her clothes, her hair. Her head had been badly smashed, you could see that, but like I told you, the car must have rolled. The rest of the car . . . it was like the flames hadn't travelled, like they hadn't had time to take hold. But that was a strange thing, you see, if her body was burned like that, if the flames had been that fierce on her body then why hadn't it spread? I think if Mr Carter and his boy hadn't arrived so prompt like, it would have done because like the sergeant said, there was fuel everywhere. You could smell it in the grass, the back seat of the car, you could see it in the stream, but Mr Carter and his son-in-law put it out. Though they'd struggled with it, the two of them had put it out completely. You could smell the fuel on the body as well. Even after the fire was extinguished, you could smell it on the seats and on the body.'

Henry didn't bother to ask the constable if he was certain. The younger man had obviously struggled with all of this – and with the casualness of the investigation that had first taken place, Henry guessed.

'Did you search the area?' he asked.

'Not immediately, sir – our concern was getting the young man out of the valley. He was unconscious, his head was bleeding, and it was clear there were bones broken. The doctor arrived, and an ambulance a little bit after. We laid him on a blanket and six of us carried him up the hill.' He laughed shortly. 'He was not a big young man, but he felt like he weighed a ton while we were trying to carry him up the hill.'

'I can imagine.' Henry looked somewhat apprehensively back the way they had come wondering if he would need carrying. He reminded himself that his legs were still perfectly sound. They just felt as though he had walked for miles. It would, he thought, take time to get his fitness back.

'By that time it was getting dark, there was only so much we could see, even with flashlights and then we got orders we were to wait for the man from London, for the inspector to come. Inspector Shelton arrived the following day and we brought him out here in the afternoon. The young woman, she was still in the car.' This was something that obviously troubled him. 'We covered everything down with tarpaulins but we thought the most important thing was to get the living out of the valley and leave the dead for after, so we left a guard of two constables overnight and then we brought Inspector Shelton straight down after lunchtime.'

'So he had seen the scene almost intact,' Henry said. 'Did he take the photographs himself?'

'He had a sergeant with him – he took the pictures. I'm sorry I don't remember his name.'

Henry tried to remember if the sergeant's name had been in the records and came to the conclusion that it definitely had not. He was momentarily irritated with himself for not asking Shelton who had gone up to Derbyshire with him. If it had been a sergeant from Central Office then he could be easily tracked down, but it was possible he had borrowed a local man as this had not been a murder investigation. That Shelton had been there at all was, as he had said, simply down to the fact that these were young people with power and money, connections and contacts, and their families had no doubt kicked up a fuss.

Stiffly, aware that if he sat down for any longer he would not get up again, Henry got to his feet. 'No doubt when the area was searched last year the foliage would have been dense,' he said, 'seeing as it was early autumn. It is sparser now; it is possible we might find something that was missed. It's worth a look. Can you show us where the young man was lying?'

The constable remembered the spot; he had re-marked it well, between two small saplings and in among fresh brambles. At this time of year the brambles were brown and perhaps less fearsome but, Henry thought, ruefully sucking his hand, they were still fierce and sharp. He pulled a fragment of cloth from a thorn and examined it carefully. It looked like blue silk and a little further on they found the remains of a woman's stocking.

'Apparently there was a picnic basket and two overnight bags in the car?' Mickey asked.

'The picnic basket was strapped to the boot, on the outside; the bags were probably inside. The boot had unlatched as the car rolled – one bag had been thrown out, the other had caught on the latch but had split and there were clothes strewn about the place. Men's clothes,' he added. 'The lady's bag, that was over there, half in the stream, just beyond where the car landed, and it had burst open, but there was still clothing in the case. It had one of those strap things, with a clasp on each side of the case when it was opened.'

'Was there a handbag, anything of that sort?' Mickey asked.

The constable thought about it then shook his head. 'I don't think so. I don't remember there being anything like that in the car, and if it had fallen out, we didn't find it.'

'How far about had things been spread?' Henry asked.

'About halfway down the hill, and as wide as that stand of silver birch over that way, and where we just sat down on those logs on this side.'

For the next twenty minutes or so they wandered along the valley floor, looking for anything that might have been hidden in the undergrowth during the first search. It was Mickey who found the compact. It was lying some distance away, open and the mirror smashed as though it had been thrown with some force against the ground. The three of them examined it where it lay before Mickey carefully scooped it up and put it in a bag.

'A brass compact, cheap and of little value,' Henry said.

'Not the kind of thing that would have been owned by Faun Moran, that's a certainty,' Mickey said. 'It's the kind of thing a working girl would buy at Woolworths.'

'You think it might belong to whoever that poor young lady was?' Constable Burton asked.

'It's entirely possible,' Henry said. 'Perhaps it is a clue to her identity.' He hoped it might be. It saddened him that so many went to their graves unknown and unmarked. Bodies pulled from the river or found dead in derelict buildings. She had to have come from somewhere, he told himself, but then, so did all of those other lost souls. Resolutely he put the thought aside. It was dusk by the time they got back to the car. It had started to rain and Henry was exhausted. He had allowed the other two to assist him on the last part of the climb, though it hurt his pride. Constable Burton, to give him his due, had been matter-of-fact about the process; Mickey had been concerned. 'You've overdone it,' he had growled. 'Tomorrow you must rest up. And we haven't finished with today yet.' There was still the visit to Fred Birch at the garage and Farmer Carter and his son-in-law. Vaguely Henry wondered if it was acceptable to ask to be left in the car while his very competent sergeant and also very competent constable took over, but he decided it probably wasn't.

The little garage-cum-filling station that belonged to Fred Birch was a couple of miles along the narrow road at the edge of the next village. He had two petrol pumps, and what would seem to be a thriving repair shop behind. A mechanic was dealing with a car lifted on to a ramp and another was tinkering with an engine that looked much more agricultural. Fred Birch himself was a little man, small and wiry with dark eyes that came alive when Henry complimented him on his business. He led them through to a tiny office, boiled an ancient kettle and made strong tea while Constable Burton explained to him what they had seen that day and what he had told these two officers from London.

'I'm told you fetched the car out of the valley,' Henry said.

'We did, yes. And a job and a half that was. Took us most of the day. We had to do it in stages, bringing it up part way and then let the winch and generator cool down before we brought in the rest. It took three of us to get it out of the beck and we pushed it as far as we could before we could fit the winch to anything. You have to understand, we got an A-frame winch and a portable generator fixed solid on the ground about halfway up the slope, then we winched the car up, locked it off so it couldn't roll back, then moved the A-frame further up and eventually we got it to the top. I wanted to do it in two halves, cut the whole bugger up and bring it up in sections, but we had our orders that we couldn't do that. The car had to be brought up in one go.'

'Orders from who?' Henry asked.

'Why, the father of the young fella that was driving it. He paid for the operation, paid for the extra generator to be brought in. I told him when he came to see me no way could we winch by hand up that slope, not and live to tell the tale. We needed power and you can't winch with a vehicle, it's not like you're pulling something on to the low-loader on the flatbed. You've seen that valley, you've seen the drop-off, so you can imagine what a tough time we had. Give him his due though, he paid for the best equipment that could be had locally and he paid us all well. I told him, the car was buggered, bring it up in bits. It was clear it would have to be written off but' – he shrugged – 'he had the money, I had the expertise, and we got the job done.'

'Where was the car taken to after that?'

'Mr Everson wanted it taken to their estate so that's what I did. Parked it up in an old barn about a mile from the house. He was there to supervise along with half a dozen of the estate workers. They got it off the truck, shut it in and to my knowledge it might still be there. I just took the rest of my pay and went.' Fred Birch paused and then said, 'He said if I went to the kitchen they'd see me fed and watered before I went on my way but' – he shrugged – 'to be truthful I just wanted to be out of there. Some places there is only grief. I saw enough grief in the war, I don't want no more of it. I tend to step away from it when I can, if you know what I mean.' He looked keenly at the two police officers and then added, 'I don't suppose you get much opportunity to step away in your job.'

'Not a lot,' Mickey said cheerfully. 'We just have to hope some good comes out of our interference.'

'And what was your impression of the damage to the car?' Henry wanted to know.

'Well, it had obviously rolled down the slope, not slid. It had turned a few times, judging by the bending and the damage. It's an open-top vehicle, so the young fella had been thrown clear, though that was strange, I'd have expected him to be further up the slope, thrown out first. You think about how it must come off the road I'd have expected the front end to drop down, being the heaviest and the back end to go somersaulting over the top of that, so the first roll, if you like, would have been more end over end than side over side, if you get my meaning. The front of the car was stoved in, the engine partly pushed back into the passenger space, so they was lucky not to be crushed. The way I figure it, they must have tipped forward, flipped and then rolled, like I said side over side and the young woman's ankle had got caught under the seat and that held her in place so she must have rolled with it all the way down the hill. Then the fire started, I suppose, when they hit the bottom.'

'But the fire was peculiarly focused,' Henry put to him.

'It seemed to me,' Fred Birch said slowly, 'and I'm no expert in this, you understand, that the fire seemed to have begun with the young lady, not with the petrol tank, which is where you would have expected. The tank had cracked, but not split open, and though there was fuel everywhere, it was not as bad as it could have been had the tank split. You could have smelled it had you been there, and arguably it's a miracle the valley wasn't burnt. In a dry season it would have been, but it had been a wet June and for that we must be thankful. Carter and his lad, they were keen to stop the fire and it's as well they did. Had they been a few minutes later, my guess is there would have been nothing they could have done except get out the way.'

'And that might have been the most sensible course of action, even so,' Mickey put in.

The three of them considered this for a moment or two, and Henry asked if there was anything else he could add but it seemed he could not. Then, since the Carters were expecting them, they went on their way.

'I always admire people that can fix things,' Mickey said. 'If I ever leave the police force, I fancy a job mechanicing.'

'It was interesting what he said, that to his eye the fire began with the woman and not with the car.'

'Interesting indeed, but I'm not sure how much further it gets us. What was also interesting is that Everson Senior wanted the car intact. Do you think he had it examined?'

'But for what? His son was blamed for driving too fast while drunk. It's an easy explanation – what reason would he have to doubt it?'

'Perhaps someone described the scene to him and cast doubt,' Mickey said. 'It's becoming clearer and clearer that someone managed that scene, just as they staged the placing of the young woman on the sand. It is as if they're leaving a trail for us.'

'A little fanciful,' Henry said. 'If someone wanted us to know something, why not just write a letter?'

'Because people never do,' Mickey told him. 'Human nature is never plain and simple. Folk always go in a roundabout way to get to where they ought to be.'

He sounded, Henry thought, quite satisfied with that fact, and Henry suspected Mickey enjoyed life's complications and would not have it any other way.

To get to the Carters' farm they had to backtrack towards the crash site, and then Constable Burton turned off into an almost invisible opening and they found themselves on a cart track. After a few hundred yards the land opened out and the farm was revealed and Henry realized that they were roughly above the crash site but higher up the hill, in fact on top of the hill. He would never have guessed that the farm could be here after the enclosure of the tight road and woodland, but this high up the land was exposed and he could imagine in winter would be bitterly cold. It was rugged land with outcroppings of stone and tough little sheep and the Carters' farm seemed built of much the same gritstone as the land they worked. Carter himself was a tall man, muscular and thickset, his son-in-law was introduced as Owen Blake, a sinewy man, obviously used to heavy labour. Henry could glimpse two women working in the backyard, hanging washing on a long line, the sheets almost dragged from their hands by the strong wind. Further down the hill he had not been aware of just how blustery the day was, or how frigid. He shivered and realized that he was being surveyed critically by Carter and a little more sympathetically by his son-in-law.

'This must be a hard land to make a living,' Henry said.

The man nodded. It seemed that he had paused in some task or other, not immediately discernible to Henry, in order to speak to them, and every attitude of his body informed the strangers that he wanted to get back to his work.

'I heard the crash. I guessed what had gone on. Stupid young fools, take that bend too fast, it's a wonder more of them have ended up in the hole.'

'So you and your son-in-law went straight down there?' Mickey asked.

'Sent the boy across fields to fetch the doctor. Me and Owen went down to take a look. On fire it was, stink of petrol all round every which where. Fire were out by the time doctor arrived. The woman were dead before we got there.'

Carter shifted from foot to foot, so impatient to be off. He must have told the story many times, Henry thought. Privately he doubted that the farmer could add much to their pool of knowledge. The son-in-law spoke for the first time. He cast a look that was a mix of determination and anxiety at his father-in-law and received a nod in return. It was clear, Henry thought, that these two men had decided what they were going to tell the strange police officers from London. He waited, feeling a little impatient now. The weariness was growing in his bones, his muscles ached and frankly he'd had enough of the day.

'She didn't die in the fire,' Owen Blake said. 'I'll tell you that for nothing. She was dead before the fire started.'

'What makes you think that?' Mickey asked him.

'Her face, her head. Bashed and broken they were. Oh, ay, you'll be telling me it happened when the car rolled down the hill.'

'That would seem likely,' Mickey pressed.

'And barely a mark on her elsewhere?'

Henry frowned. 'How could you tell that? She was on fire.'

'And we took a good look once the fire was put out. True, she was burnt, burnt badly, but you could see the marks on her face, like someone had taken something hard and heavy and taken care to bash in her mouth and nose and cheeks and eyes. Her hands too, broken up and twisted and not from the fire.'

'Did you mention this to anyone else? What did the doctor think?'

'Dr Craddock lost interest once he discovered she was dead and paid more attention to the young man. After all, he was still living. But he knew we had a point. We talked about it after. We tried to tell that inspector when he came up but he didn't want to know. Even when Dr Craddock talked to him, he didn't want to know.'

'We need to speak to Dr Craddock,' Henry said.

'You'll be lucky,' Carter said. 'Died last November. Heart attack. Damned fool should have retired long since, we were all telling him. He was a good man was Dr Craddock. Not uppity like some, didn't think he was better than the rest of us. Grew up in the village.'

'And his replacement?' Mickey asked innocently.

'Come from Sheffield,' Carter said, as though that was explanation enough.

They left the Carters and Burton drove them back to the inn where they were staying. Henry was aware of Mickey regarding him somewhat anxiously. 'You need to rest tomorrow.'

'Tomorrow we go and see the family of Malcolm Everson,' Henry reminded him, but he had fallen asleep in the car and didn't object when Mickey demanded that he get into a hot bath once they arrived back at their lodgings at the inn. The hot water had done something to relieve the aches, but the idea of traipsing downstairs for dinner seemed too much. He was profoundly relieved when a little later Mickey arrived with sandwiches and soup and hot tea, having sweet-talked the landlady into allowing them to eat in their rooms.

'Sometimes being a police detective from London has its advantages,' he told his boss cheerfully.

Sometimes, Henry thought, it was just an advantage to be Mickey Hitchens. He had a talent for dealing with members of the public, and for charming landladies.

'I am bone tired,' Henry confessed. 'Even my brain is bone tired.'

'You're sure to be,' Mickey told him. 'But we've had a good day, a day of uncovering more of this mystery, and we have our first little inkling as to who this young woman in the car might have been.'

'If the powder compact was indeed hers.' Henry as usual felt the need to play devil's advocate.

'And the likelihood of some other young woman having lost her compact in that steep valley?'

'Small, I agree, small. What is in play here, Mickey? None of it makes a hap'orth of sense.'

Mickey had set the tray with sandwiches and soup on Henry's bed and a tea tray, brought in by an accompanying barmaid, on the chest of drawers. 'Eat,' he said. 'Feed that brain of yours. The ham is good, the soup is not bad from the smell of it and I don't know about you but I am well in need of tea.'

He had to agree with that, Henry thought. He picked up his soup and began to eat. It was more stew than soup, thick with vegetables and served in a deep, rounded bowl that felt comforting in the hands. He watched as Mickey dipped a slice of sandwich into the broth and then tried it himself, deciding that it was an excellent combination, and slowly felt some of the weariness ebbing away and a little of his usual alertness returning.

'I was impressed with the constable,' Mickey said.

'He's a good man,' Henry agreed. 'Observant. For that matter, all the witnesses were observant. I'm not surprised that DI Shelton ignored them all. Any one of them could have run rings round him in terms of intelligence. Experience too. That would have hurt his pride. So how does this move things forward?'

Mickey took another bite of his sandwich and chewed thoughtfully before saying, 'I think they're right – it seems to centre around this young woman. In fact, around the two young women. The car went off the road and rolled down the hill. Whether it dived nose first or not initially is a moot point. The fact is it rolled and ended up in the stream. It spilt fuel, but not as much as it could have done. There was, it seems, a crack in the fuel tank, but not a complete break, so enough to smell strong but not so much that the fire spread. And it seems to me that in the June heat, the smell would be stronger especially trapped in that tight space at the valley floor.'

'It's a good point,' Henry agreed. 'But the woman was on fire, and if not set ablaze by the crash then what? A woman on fire would scream, if she was conscious, of course, but from what we have heard of the head injuries it's likely she was not. It is likely that either as a cause of the crash or some other means she had already lost consciousness and I suppose that is some mercy.'

'It is definitely possible she was even dead already,' Mickey agreed. 'I'm inclined to believe Carter and his son-in-law. That the injuries may have been inflicted prior to the crash, that the fire was intended to cover everything up. That perhaps nobody expected Carter and his son-in-law to arrive as quickly as they did, or at all. According to their initial statements, and from what they confirmed today, they were down the track and down the hill in very swift order. There *was* a blaze, the car was ablaze, or at least the front seat was and the rest soon would have been. They thought quickly and acted quickly and the fire was put out. It seems to me that no one could have anticipated their presence. That the two of them were proverbial spanners in the proverbial works.'

'And even had anyone been aware of the possibility of Carter and his son-in-law turning up, I doubt any account of them would have been taken. A farmer and his son-in-law, common men according to the thinking of many, not blessed with intelligence and observational skills or courage.'

Mickey laughed and then was silent while he finished his soup and sandwiches. Henry, realizing that he was in fact very hungry, demolished his share and then poured them both more tea, topping up the pot from the hot water jug on the tray.

Mickey had fished the powder compact out of his pocket and it now lay on top of the paper bag he had used to house it. It was a brass compact, rounded and of the size to fit in a woman's palm, a band of engine turning was the only decoration and it had a certain elegance to it even though it had been cheaply made. The mirror was broken, the sifter and pad lost, though there were still traces of the loose powder under the rim. Henry sniffed at it; the familiar violet scent of orris root still clung faintly even after all this time and weathering. The compact had landed upside down under a bush and that no doubt had sheltered it from the worst of the environment.

'The hinge had been broken,' he said, noting a little patch of rust against the brass. 'Look, a piece of wire, a pin perhaps, has been pushed through and the end curled over to make the repair. Whatever was used, it has rusted.'

'So a treasured item but a makeshift repair. Mind you how many of us have done that same thing? We have fixed something to make it secure and usable and perhaps taken months before we have fixed it better.'

'And no handbag,' Henry said. 'Unlike our poor unfortunate

Faun Moran, the rest of this girl's most personal possessions seem to have been taken away. Though I suppose anything else she had might have been removed with the car.'

He doubted that, though. She had been discarded. Henry felt this instinctively. Discarded in such a way that nobody would be able to identify her. Conversely, someone wanted to be certain that when it came to Faun Moran's turn to be cast aside, it would not be without her name.

As though Mickey had been following his thoughts, which knowing Mickey he probably had, his sergeant said, 'Even in death there is no equality, whatever your average preacher might say. At least we know who our body on the beach is. This poor little scrap is totally anonymous.'

'So we will have to give her name back to her,' Henry said.

EIGHT

Faun, October

T he first thing I remember was waking up in this room
and not knowing where I was. I felt so sick. There
was a young girl sitting beside my bed. She looked
as scared as I felt, even before I remembered what had
happened.

She stood and slipped an arm around my shoulders and put
a glass to my lips. Drink this, miss, she said, it will make you
feel better. I'm ashamed to say I didn't even ask her what it
was. Then she laid me down again and tucked the blankets
up to my chin and I remember thinking that she was just a
child. Why was a child looking after me? Why did I need
looking after anyway? I must have muttered something because
she told me, 'You've been poorly, miss, very poorly and
the master says you need rest and quiet.'

I saw her looking round this little room as though she
was momentarily surprised that I should be here and not
in one of the many guest rooms, but then she said, 'Master
said this was the quietest place in the house. You'll not be
disturbed here, miss, and no one can hear you if you have
bad dreams and cry out, so you're not to be worried about
that.'

I must have slept again and when I woke up she was no
longer there. Pat, I have never felt so alone or so afraid.
Not even when I saw that poor broken body in the car and
I realized that might just as soon have been me.

I got up off the bed and I tried the door and I realized I
could not get out. I was a prisoner here. And Pat, I was so
very afraid.

Saturday 11 January

Henry woke and stretched, feeling desperately stiff and appallingly uncomfortable. His shoulder ached and so did his head and the thought of another busy day stretching out in front of him filled him with a kind of despair.

Shaking himself out of the mood, he washed and dressed and went down to breakfast. Mickey was already there, sitting in a corner of what would be the public bar later in the day, his legs stretched out before the fire, a steaming cup of tea on the table beside him and the local newspapers piled high close at hand. Henry was unsurprised to see that their presence had been the cause of headlines. The link to Faun Moran had been made, of course, and Henry was amused to find that he had apparently 'come out of retirement' in order to lead the investigation.

Breakfast arrived – eggs and bacon, sausage and fried bread. Henry ate slowly; Mickey did not. Mickey dived in with abandon and when his boss seemed likely not to need his other slice of fried bread he helped himself to that too.

'Are you leaving that bacon?'

'No, I'm merely making it available to you.'

'Good of you,' Mickey said, folding the rasher between the last slice of fried bread and eating it with obvious relish.

Amused, Henry sat back and watched him. He was aware that this level of familiarity was frowned upon by many of their colleagues, particularly the senior ones, but the relation-ship he and his sergeant had went far beyond that of chief inspector and sergeant. Henry counted Mickey as at least his equal both as investigator and as man. 'So,' he said, 'today we go out to visit the family of Malcolm Everson to see if we can ascertain what happened to the car and the luggage after it was taken from the crash site. And *why* it was taken from the crash site. And we demand to be allowed to see Malcolm Everson. I don't frankly care how ill the young man is. He is a key witness and his family can only protect him for so long. Two young women are dead and for my money both have been murdered.'

'You will find no argument from me,' Mickey told him. 'If the family don't cooperate then we must appeal to a judge, see if we could be granted an order to speak to Malcolm Everson. He must know something. His amnesia, or whatever it is, is far too convenient.'

He reached over to the stack of newspapers and produced a map. 'I borrowed this from the landlady,' he said. 'I found myself lost in all the twists and turns yesterday and I had no clear image in my mind of the relationship between the crash site and the Belmonts' house or of how far it might be, how long it would have taken to drive.'

Henry nodded. He'd been wondering the same thing. He took out his notebook and examined the notes he had taken – elements that had particularly struck him from the reports he had read. 'According to the witnesses at the house, Malcolm Everson and Faun Moran left the party at around four thirty on the Saturday afternoon. The house party had begun on the Friday evening, then begun again in earnest after lunch on the Saturday. Everson had arrived that morning and Faun Moran been a guest since the night before.'

'So, they left at four thirty, they drove to the crash site, the car went off the road and plummeted into the valley. Though I'd like to call it a ravine, considering how much my legs and back still hurt from clambering down and then up again.'

'Ravine it is, then. And Carter and Blake, our father and his son-in-law, they reckon to have heard the crash at around a quarter to six in the evening, just as they were preparing to go in to eat.'

'So, that means it took them over an hour to get from the Belmonts' house to the crash site.' Mickey cleared their plates from the table, taking them and the map across to the bar where their landlady was preparing for the business day. They spoke for several minutes and when he returned Mickey had marked the map with a pencilled cross. 'I doubt either you or I could work out where the Carters' farm might be,' he said. 'But Mrs Cross knows all about the crash and the Carters and was able to help us out. Now, the Belmonts' house is here.' He jabbed at the page with his finger. 'The crash site is hereabouts. There are three ways of leaving the estate: the private station, which is where we arrived, and two tracks or driveways. Look, you can see them on the map, but only one apparently is paved and used for motor vehicles. As our chauffeur told us yesterday, they would have taken this route out on to the main road, such as it is.'

Henry studied the map, following the route with his finger. 'The road to the crash site is, as we discovered yesterday, twisting and steep, but it's not more than five miles from the house. The Aston Martin Everson was driving is a vehicle built for speed, and I cannot imagine that a young man like Malcolm Everson would have driven slowly. He would have seen the steepness and the twisting road as a challenge. What young man does not wish to show off his driving prowess to a young woman he admires? So why did it take them over an hour to reach the spot where the car left the road?'

'That is if the witnesses remember correctly,' Mickey reminded him. 'Eyewitnesses are notoriously bad at remembering times unless they have reason to look at their watches.'

Henry thought about it for a moment and then said, 'Witnesses from the party remember the young couple being in the hallway and leaving by the front door. From what I remember of yesterday there is an impressive longcase clock standing in the hall. Presuming it was working, and it certainly was yesterday, it would have chimed the half-hour. So it is quite possible that our witnesses at the Belmonts' house party were accurate in their statements. Carter would have been used to doing everything at certain times of the day. Farmers, I imagine, are creatures of routine with livestock to feed and tasks to attend to. There would be a rhythm to their lives. He and his boy would know when they usually go in to eat supper. I doubt their recollection of time would have been much astray either.'

'You make a good case,' Mickey told him. 'Everson and the girl could have stopped somewhere on the way, of course, but there would not have been enough time to have a picnic, if that was their intention. And we drove that road yesterday

– there were few suitable stopping places if that had been their intention. I noted a few small laybys, carved into the rock, to allow for easy passage should two large vehicles meet, but not much else. It is not a road that invites a pause on a journey. From what I saw there was not even what you'd call a view. Just a steep slope, cliffs on one side going up and another equally steep going down.'

Henry nodded agreement. 'But even driving slowly, in bad winter weather, I doubt it would have taken so much time. And this was not bad weather. It was June, it was still light, and as a frequent visitor to the Belmonts' house I imagine Everson was familiar with the route.'

Mickey glanced up as the outer door swung open. 'And here's our driver for today,' he said. Henry was pleased to see that once again it was Constable Burton. He would, Henry thought, be a good person to ask about the route and how long it might take to drive on an ordinary June evening.

Constable Burton's opinion matched their own and he offered to drive them both from the crash site back to the Belmonts' house so they could examine the route later, if there was time.

'What do you know about the Eversons?' Mickey asked. 'Are they a local family?'

'The grandfather bought the estate, I suppose about fifty years ago. There are several farms, some forestry, a lot of tied cottages and I think they've some involvement in the weaving. We have a lot of textile mills around here, though not as many now as we did have even fifty years back. He doesn't have a bad reputation as a landlord, but then again he doesn't have a good one either. The family donate to charity on a regular basis, because that's expected round here, all the landowners do. Mr George Everson lives on the land full-time, like his father did before him but the rumours say that Malcolm Everson was not so keen. Not the farming type, or the business type, so his father had sent him away to study law. Fortunately there is an elder brother who seems cut from the old cloth. I've met the brother, Mr Ford Everson and I have to say, sir, I don't *dislike* him. He's quite a bit older than

Mr Malcolm, and he's a local magistrate, so I've had dealings with him time to time. He's not a man to put on false graces, if you get my meaning. Some might call him blunt, but he's quite a decent sort as these things go.'

Mickey reflected the previous day that this young man would probably not have been so outspoken but they had encouraged his observations and his confidence had grown and this local information was certainly proving useful. He was potential detective material, Mickey thought.

At first the journey had taken them along a road that was similar to yesterday's, rocky and wooded and narrow and with a steep drop-off. Then they found themselves descending into a broad and sunlit valley. The sunlight was still winter cold but Mickey could imagine what it must look like in spring and summer, even in autumn when the trees turned red and gold and the sparkle bounced from the water. Surrounding the valley were high hills, not covered with trees but with what he guessed must be heath and heather. It looked barren to Mickey's eye but he supposed there was a wild and severe kind of beauty to it.

'How far away is the Everson place?' he asked.

'Another seven miles, going up there.' Constable Burton gestured towards the moorland. 'Good views from up there,' he added, 'but it's mostly shooting country, all private owner- ship. You get walkers here in the valley but that's as far as they go. There's some Bolshie talk with the tourists and with some of the locals that they should be allowed to go up on to the moor, but I can't see that happening, not in my lifetime.'

Mickey wasn't quite sure why anyone would want to, but then he liked tramping along city streets and he presumed that not everybody would see the appeal of that either.

He glanced across at Henry who was busy following their route on the map and getting his bearings. 'How far is the Belmonts' house from the Eversons?' he asked.

Henry pointed out their respective positions. 'I suppose about twenty miles by road,' he said. 'I presume all the local families, the landowning families, I mean, are known to one another?' he asked Constable Burton.

'Most are close,' he said, and there was an edge to his tone that spoke of unvoiced disapproval. 'As the landlords go, like I said, Everson isn't bad and their estate is one of the largest not in titled hands. The Belmont place is posh, but it's not really that big. They don't farm or anything like that – they keep it as a country retreat and employ a lot of the local girls when they need extra hands for parties and that sort of thing. They get people come up from London a couple of times a month, I suppose. Not so much in the summer, I think, as the family go away for a month or two around July and August. But they usually spend Christmas at the big house and, like I say, their house parties might happen a couple of times a month through the spring and autumn.'

'And I suppose the local constabulary is very aware of the comings and goings?' Mickey asked.

'It pays to be.' Constable Burton hesitated.

'Come on, lad, what were you about to say?'

'It's not that there's any harm in the young people that come up, it's just that they have no understanding of the countryside or of the feelings of local people. They go tramping across the fields, upsetting the livestock and flattening the crops. Driving too fast, and I have to say often while under the influence. And you see the roads round here, you can guess how dangerous it might be, especially in the winter. It's a regular occurrence, having to pull some car out of the field when it's gone off the road and barged through a hedge or worse, demolished a dry-stone wall. And neither of those take five minutes to repair so the farmer has to cobble something together so the livestock don't go wandering. And if you know sheep, you know they're just woolly Houdinis. This is not the first accident we had on that bit of road where we were yesterday. Or the first fatality. But it's like they come in as though they own the place and have no feeling for the locals, or at least for those that aren't moneyed. Not that I want to speak out of turn, and I know I am, but you did ask.'

'We have trouble with the same set in London,' Mickey said. 'Bright young things driving their cars too fast in races across the city. Taking part in treasure hunts and scavenger hunts, and they don't seem to care whether they're on private

property or not. I agree, most of the time they're not meaning
any harm, they're just thoughtless and rich and it never occurs
to them that they might be causing trouble with their practical
jokes or their brand of fun. But I can imagine it must rankle
in a place like this.'

'And did you ever run across Faun Moran or Malcolm
Everson when you were dealing with troublemakers?' Henry
asked.

'Not especially that I remember,' Constable Burton said.
Henry got the distinct impression that he was merely being
tactful with the 'not especially'.

The Everson house was old and grey and ivy-clad and
compared quite dramatically to the stylish building they had
visited the day before of the Belmonts. They drove down an
avenue of trees and glimpsed the ubiquitous sheep, for much
of the land seemed open and heather-covered and Henry
wondered what on earth they could grow there, or how the
estate made its living. He remembered what Constable Burton
had said about this being shooting land. Did they have grouse
here? Pheasants? Henry was not particularly au fait with
country pursuits.

A number of barns and outbuildings dotted the landscape,
also stone-built and around which seemed to be more cultivated
land. The house itself had gardens beyond and what looked
like an orchard. Constable Burton dropped them at the front
and drove around the back of the house. He had been instructed
to gather any gossip he could as no doubt their presence would
have stimulated a lot of interest among the staff and the newspaper reports would have aroused curiosity in even the most
proper cook or butler. The staff of a house like this often knew
more about the business of the owner than any householder
would be willing to admit and Henry had no doubt that
Constable Burton was perfectly capable of extracting any such
information that might be available.

They were led into a study that was warm, quite dark,
formal but still inviting. It contrasted dramatically with
the bright little room that the Belmonts used as their private
sitting area. A young man came in to greet them and

introduced himself as Ford Everson, Malcolm's elder brother. He looked to be in his mid-thirties, was tall and straight and had a very direct way of looking at the visitors as though summing them up and, Henry thought, appraising what trouble they might bring.

'My father was called away on business. I hope I'll do. I probably know as much as he does about this whole sordid affair. But I don't know what else I can tell you. We've made statement after statement, been through the dreadful business with the coroner.' He shrugged and spread his hands as though pained and eager to be disposed of the whole matter. 'I understand that Mr Caius Moran is refusing to speak to the police,' he added. 'That he simply wants this unknown woman exhumed from the family tomb so that his daughter can be interred and the matter closed.'

This was news to Henry, but he merely nodded.

'This is a difficult time for all concerned,' Mickey intoned sympathetically.

A knock at the door announced the arrival of coffee. Just coffee, Henry noted, not the option of tea or cake and sandwiches. Everson was bound to be polite but he had no expectation of them pushing the limits of his politeness.

'We understand you had the car brought here.' Henry got straight to the point.

'We did. What of it?'

'And the luggage that was in the car?'

Everson shrugged. 'I imagine if it was in the car then that's where it still is. We didn't want the car left to rot, it seemed . . .' He paused as though unsure of how to express his thoughts, but in the end he said, 'Seemed disrespectful to the dead girl. Of course, at that time we thought it was Faun, and we didn't want it picked clean by sightseers and voyeurs. I imagine the men who winched the car from the ravine also gathered together whatever belongings they could find and put them back in the car.'

'Sightseers would have to be quite determined,' Mickey commented. 'It is not an easy location to access.'

'Apparently not. I didn't go there. I arranged for the matter to be taken care of and it was, very capably by a man who

owns a local repair place.' He frowned, as though struggling
to remember. 'A Mr Birch, I believe. He brought the car here
and parked it in one of the old barns that is no longer in
use and that's where it remains.'

'We would like to see it,' Henry said.

'For what reason?'

'I'm sure you understand, now that we know that Faun
Moran's body was not the one that was found in the car,
we are investigating two cases of murder. That of Miss
Moran and of the poor unfortunate that was in your brother's
car.'

Ford Everson sighed but accepted the inevitable. 'I'll get
someone to take you to it,' he said. 'Or to give directions to
your driver, it's not far. I'm presuming there's nothing more?'

He hadn't even bothered to pour the coffee, Henry
noted. He was eager to be done with them. 'If there is then
we will contact you,' Henry told him.

Everson glanced at his watch. 'You must excuse me. Please
drink your coffee. I will send word that you are ready for your
driver and that he needs to be given directions to the barn.
Drop the key at the gamekeeper's cottage, it is adjacent to the
barn, you may just post it through his letterbox. He will know
what to do with it. Now, if you will excuse me.'

Whether they would or not he left. Henry watched as he
opened the heavy study door, not bothering to close it behind
him. He heard Mickey pouring coffee, Mickey never being
one to pass up what smelt like very good coffee. He handed
Henry a cup. A woman's voice attracted Henry's attention and
as Henry watched a girl, perhaps in her early twenties, came
down the stairs and spoke to Ford Everson.

'I saw a car pull up. Who is here?'

'Nothing to concern you. Just the police following up on
enquiries. You know, after this other business.'

He marched on past her and she turned and looked towards
the study, her head slightly on one side as she considered the
figure of Henry Johnstone. He felt himself thoroughly scrutin-
ized though not judged, he thought. She was merely curious.
She had blue eyes and very dark, bobbed hair and was dressed
for riding. She smiled at him and then went on her way.

'That must be Violet Everson,' Mickey said. 'The younger sister. I believe she was on the guest list for the ill-fated party.'

A moment later the butler returned to tell them that their car was waiting and the driver had been given instructions for how to get to the barn. He handed Henry the key, a large and somewhat rusted affair. Looking at it, Henry found himself hoping that the locks would still be working.

'I hope you fared better than we did,' Mickey said. 'We were offered coffee but no time to drink it and a brief audience with Mr Ford Everson, but it was clear he did not want to remain in our company for longer than was absolutely necessary.'

Constable Burton looked rather pleased with himself. 'I had a nice mug of tea and a piece of cake,' he said. 'And apparently Mr Everson is not happy about this new direction the enquiry's taken. He believes it might upset his younger brother and it has certainly upset their father. He's gone down to London, with a view to going anywhere he doesn't have to deal with the police. Cook seems to think that he feels the family's being brought into disrepute, that the inquest was bad enough and now they are to be dragged through the mud again. Apparently several members of staff have already left, because what happens above stairs it seems impacts on what happens below stairs and they don't want their good reputation to be risked.'

Mickey laughed and then realized that Burton was serious.

'No one wants to be judged to have been in service at a disorderly house,' the constable said. 'And I think in these parts a disorderly house probably doesn't mean what you think it means down in London. Apparently they have no end of trouble hanging on to decent staff over at the Belmonts' house and that's why they bring in local girls to help out when they have guests. The rumour is they're both short-staffed and short on cash and of course the girls just get an hourly rate, no bed and board, no commitment on either side.'

'Interesting,' Mickey said. 'And yet they still host lavish house parties.'

'Appearance is everything for some families,' Henry reminded him. 'How did the Wall Street crash and the London stock market fiasco affect them, is that known?'

'It's no secret it affected a lot of the families round here, but no one talks about it. Many of the estates dismissed staff, there's a lot of land been quietly put up for sale. But the parties still go on and the houseguests still arrive weekend after weekend.'

There was an air of desperation about all this, Henry thought. He thought about the way that his sister and brother-in-law had sold the London house and other properties and retreated to the coast. Cynthia had just been quite relieved that they *could* sell their way out of debt and much of what was left she now personally owned or was in trust for their children. They had spoken recently of Albert reviving his business prospects and Cynthia had sounded quite hopeful. Henry knew that they had been incredibly lucky not to lose more, and that their good fortune had largely been due to Cynthia's wisdom and financial acumen. But it had still been a tough time. The investigation that he had been involved in before Christmas had highlighted for him just how many bankruptcies and how much desperation the financial extremes in both London and New York had brought to those who had thought themselves secure.

'That must be the barn,' Mickey said.

Burton stopped the car in front of a large stone-built building with an almost intact roof and two small but broken windows. The doors were locked and the key did turn in the ancient lock, but discerning how they barely hung on their hinges and how rotten the wood had become Henry didn't consider them to be of much value in terms of security. They opened the doors wide, so that the grey winter light could filter in and Burton brought flashlights from the car. They needed them in the dimness.

The car stood in the centre of the large barn, broken and disconsolate. The windscreen had been torn away and the paintwork displayed the evidence of damage caused by rock and tree roots and fire. Slowly and meticulously Henry and Mickey began to examine this melancholy crime scene, now ripped from its context. Burton stood and watched them with interest, occasionally asking questions. The murder bag sat at his feet and from time to time Mickey asked for something to be retrieved from it. Camera, evidence bags, the measuring tape.

'You can see where the fire began and how it spread,' Henry said. 'It did not begin in the engine or the fuel tank. The seat of the fire is exactly that – the front passenger seat. This is burnt through to the springs beneath and the scorching has spread up the back and along the inside of the door. When it crashed down the hill the seat frame was damaged and the seat itself pushed forward and down, which I suppose is how the girl's ankle came to be trapped beneath it and why she was not flung from the car.'

He stood back and surveyed the damage, not from the flames but that which had been caused by the car's journey into the ravine. It had received crushing injuries, scratches and gores, deep tears of the upholstery. 'Now I look at the car, what strikes me is how Everson survived. How he was thrown out with, in reality, so little injury. And for that matter how the girl was not. Even if her ankle had become trapped. Would that have been enough to keep her in her seat? The entire chassis of the car appears to have been bent. If you look along the line it is warped and twisted completely out of shape.'

'Could that have happened when they pulled it back on to the road?' Burton asked.

'I doubt it. The damage to the front end almost certainly did – you can see where they've attached the chains and straps and I'm guessing that added to the damage to the front axle. You can see here where the straps have rubbed.'

'And the lack of fire damage is itself extraordinary,' Mickey added. 'Any fool could have seen that, even DI Shelton.'

'To have not seen it, he would have to have been looking the other way throughout his so-called investigation,' Henry said coldly. A thought struck him and he glanced at Constable Burton. 'Is it possible the Eversons put pressure on him, on Shelton, I mean, not to look too closely? Is that something that is likely? You understand the politics of this place, so is that possible?'

Burton looked uncomfortable but nodded. 'I was told that he was brought in because the young people were important, belonged to good families, important families, but I imagine those same families would be loath to have too much scandal attached to their names. Bad enough that young Mr Everson might have been drinking and crashed the car, and that killed the girl, but if it looked out of order in other ways then it may be that they'd rather had it covered up and hoped it went away. And it would have done if Miss Moran hadn't been found and identified.'

'Possibly so,' Henry said.

'Mr Caius Moran has a reputation for getting his own way,' Mickey suggested. 'It's possible the pressure came from him rather than the Eversons. He believed his daughter to have been killed in very unfortunate circumstances, and she was known to be something of a wild child, wilful and disobedient according to some. Perhaps he did not want anybody looking too closely into his daughter's life after she had met her death.'

'On balance I find that more likely,' Henry agreed. 'But whatever the cause, this was not investigated fully and now we have lost half a year of time.' He glanced around the barn. 'Ford Everson said the suitcases were probably here. Ah, it looks as though they are over there.'

On what was left of the workbench were three objects. A wicker picnic basket, which from the outside looked oddly untouched by its experiences, a small blue suitcase and a Gladstone bag. The suitcase and the bag were open and clothing and other personal items had been rammed carelessly inside, together with twigs and dried leaves. The clothing smelled musty as though they had been soaked in the stream and then pushed back into the bags while still damp. Henry poked about inside and then made a decision. 'These will come with us,' he said.

'That won't please the Eversons,' Mickey commented.

Henry shrugged, unconcerned. He opened the picnic basket. Inside were broken plates, cutlery and a selection of small metal sandwich boxes. Mickey withdrew one of these and carefully opened it. The remains of food inside had rotted and mouldered. The two thermos flasks, when he lifted them, rattled, the glass liner broken, though it sounded as though they were still full of liquid.

Henry and Mickey took a last look at the car while Burton placed the suitcase and Gladstone bag in their own vehicle and then they dropped the key through the letterbox of the gamekeeper's cottage, as per instructions, and went off on their way.

A telegram awaited them on their return to the inn. It was from Cynthia. Henry was aware of Mickey watching him anxiously as he read it through. Telegrams too often brought bad news. But this was useful, helpful. 'She's somehow managed to arrange for us to see Malcolm Everson,' Henry said, handing his sergeant the flimsy scrap of paper.

'Just how did she do that?'

'I think she may be acquainted with Everson's sister but Cynthia has her own networks and methods, as you know. I'm just grateful that she has.'

'Tomorrow afternoon,' Mickey said. 'At two, so we'll need to arrange transport. Best try and get hold of our constable Burton and tell him that his services are required.'

Vic

The first time Faun visited Ben's home, I had collected her in the car from the home of a mutual friend. He could see the frisson of excitement in her eyes, the knowledge that she should not be going unchaperoned and friendless into the house of the bachelor, a bachelor much older than she was and much more experienced. But for her it was an adventure and she was never one to turn down adventure.

For most of the journey she had settled in the middle of the back seat, though she did not want to be seen and the day had been cold so she had wrapped a blanket around her knees and pulled her coat tight, but as they drove through

the gates she moved over so that she could look out of the
window.

'What's the house like?'

'You'll see for yourself in a few minutes.'

'I know, but tell me.'

She had looked so anxious that it had made him laugh. It
was as though the enormity of the situation suddenly hit her.
'It's big, it's red brick, and was built about 200 years ago,
but you'll be glad to know that the plumbing is modern. He
doesn't use the whole house – it's too big for one person
and so there are rooms that have been covered down with
dust sheets and not opened up in about ten years. His father
didn't use them either. It's a shame. It would be a wonderful
house to have parties in, but Ben doesn't really fancy all of
that.'

'He likes going to parties though,' she objected.

'He likes going to other people's parties. That way he can
leave whenever he wants and does not have to play host. He
gets bored easily with all the noise and the chatter and people
drinking too much and behaving like complete idiots. It amuses
him for a while, I think, but that's about all.'

She laughed then. 'You make him sound utterly frightful
and I know he's not. I even got him to dance.'

She had indeed, Vic thought. He was saved from the bother
of further conversation because as they rounded a bend the
house came into view. It was true what he had told her about
rooms not being used. An entire wing had been closed down
and fires lit only to air the place once a week, but it was
still an impressive place and all the lights at the front of
the house were on so that it glowed like an exotic piece
of jewellery, the stained glass of the upper windows and a
large arched window above the door casting broken rainbows
out on to the drive.

'Oh, but it's beautiful,' she said.

And he knew that she was imagining herself mistress of
such a place. Free from her father, free from anybody that
could boss her around. And, he thought, given time she would
probably make a good hostess, even a good mother, a good
wife. But what she didn't understand was that Ben Caxton

was looking for none of those things. Other women had imagined themselves in this position – Ben Caxton's favourite, Ben Caxton's wife – but they had all been disappointed, some far more than others.

Ben must have seen the headlights sweeping down the drive because he was on the steps waiting for them. He came down, helped Faun from the car and led her into the hall with its marble floor and fine statuary.

'Welcome to my home,' he said, and Vic watched them both, watched his employer playing his game and innocent little Faun falling for every word.

NINE

Faun, November

My only comfort is little Martha. She is not yet fifteen and is so small for her age and such a little bird, so fragile and timid. She has been told that I am sick in the head, that I don't know what I'm saying and that my family have abandoned me. That they wanted me committed to an asylum but that HE stepped in and took over my care and protection.

So completely does Martha believe this tale that it is unassailable. I have done my best but of course anything I say just encourages her belief in my insanity and her master's goodness. But she is also a kind little soul. The master has told her that I must not tax my mind but I eventually managed to persuade her that if I had pen and paper, so that I could write down my thoughts and what she sees as my fantasies, I might be able to get them out of my head and I might be somewhat healed by this. So, bless her little heart, she contrived to procure what I had asked for and without telling her infernal master.

She found me a pencil and a stack of scraps and bits of paper which I suspect she has stolen from the wastepaper baskets and the kitchen bins. But I am so very grateful for even this small favour. I know she must have taken risks and that her loyalties must have been so divided. She is such a good little soul. I know she is unable to believe that a man who has always treated her with kindness could be the monster I have claimed.

She prattles at me. I welcome it. She tells me of life below stairs. Of the cook housekeeper, Mrs Gammon – a very appropriate name for a cook – and how she trains young girls for a life of service. Martha is orphaned as apparently are all the young servants taken into this house. I can't help but wonder

*if he takes advantage of this and how many of them actually
do end up in other households.*

*Martha is a ginger-haired, freckled little thing, with grey
eyes and a really lovely smile. It does me good to think about
her and not have to think purely about my own situation. She
says the cook is kind, that she teaches them well and does not
demand to see their blooded clouts each month. Pat, I can't
imagine having to show evidence that I'm not pregnant each
and every month. Can you imagine that? Apparently someone
told Martha that this might happen and she admits that she
was 'ever so scared'.*

*Poor sweet little thing. She can't imagine what it means to
be truly afraid and I hope she never does.*

*I am afraid for my very life. When he first suggested this
plan I expected to be here, as his guest, only for the shortest
time. We planned to give my father a shock, that was all, to
let him know that he could not continue to treat me so unfairly.
He would be worried if I disappeared, Ben said, then when I
appeared again, safe and well, he would just be so relieved
that he would . . . But Ben cheated me and I believed him.
Believed him, and now I'm come to this. I do not believe that
I will survive, and I have come to believe that I am not the
first to have been imprisoned in this house. Perhaps in this
very room.*

*Martha tells me that she will be leaving for another house-
hold just before Christmas. If I am still alive, then I will miss
her dreadfully. She tells me that the girls always leave this
place with a decent winter coat, three pairs of woollen stockings and a housewife fitted out with darning wool and needles
and all the other requisites. She has so little that this all seems
like treasure to her and I must admit that I envy her. I would
spend a lifetime on my knees scrubbing floors if it meant
getting out of here.*

Sunday 12 January

The previous evening they had spent time examining the
contents of the Gladstone bag and the suitcase to come to no

firm conclusions as to who the owners had been. The Gladstone bag contained two shirts, a pair of trousers and one of a pair of cufflinks. It also contained a woman's scarf, green and geometric in design but as the woman's suitcase contained three pairs of men's socks – 'Why three?' Mickey wanted to know – this was likely to be the result of the speed with which everything had been scooped up and shoved inside one or other of the available pieces of luggage. The quantity of leaves, now dried and shrivelled, clumps of grass and bits of bramble spoke not just of the haste with which everything had been gathered but also probably the breadth of land over which it had been spread. This could have been useful information had it been collected and studied more carefully at the time, Henry thought, but not now.

The contents of the suitcase were a little more interesting. A dress, suitable for evening wear but not expensive. It was of the sort advertised for mail order in the Sunday newspapers, pretty and respectable but of inexpensive cloth. A pair of slacks made of decent quality wool which had been darned at pocket and ankle. Skilfully and nearly invisibly mended, he guessed, using threads drawn from the fabric turned at the hem, as he recalled both his mother and his sister doing, though whoever had done this lacked such fine skill as Henry's mother had possessed. Her invisible darns had been just that. Additionally there was a woman's blouse, another scarf, this one blue chiffon and a lightweight cardigan.

'What strikes you, Mickey?' Henry asked.

'No nightclothes,' Mickey said. 'No underclothes either. While I agree, if this was a romantic liaison, the nightclothes may well have been shed, but most people in my experience at least go through the motions of getting dressed for bed.'

Both suitcase and Gladstone bag were now back in the police vehicle, ably driven by Constable Burton, and all were headed for the exclusive sanatorium which had been home to Mal Everson for the last six months.

Willow Haven was some fifteen miles from where they were staying. It was fortunate, Henry thought, that this sanatorium was still in Derbyshire, and he assumed this was because after the accident it had been easier to remove Mal Everson to somewhere close rather than to shift him back to London or the other family property in Hampshire.

It was close to a spa town, Constable Burton had told them, popular with the 'rich and weary' in search of a rest cure. From his tone Henry gathered that Burton had a similar view of the rich and privileged as had Mickey. He had little patience with their complaints.

Willow Haven had clearly been a family home at some point, one owned by someone wealthy enough and, in Henry's view, tasteless enough to have added two massive wings to the Georgian frontage. It was set in parkland and here and there Henry spied solitary figures walking slowly and purpose-fully as though the exercise had been prescribed. In the summer no doubt they sat outside, bathing in the sun and drinking the spa water. Such places had never seemed to Henry to be particularly restful – not that he had encountered one in any meaningful way. He had certainly never partaken of such a rest cure.

There were four other cars parked outside, spaces defined by white-painted, numbered blocks which sat next to a stern notice informing visitors that they must keep off the grass and please use the path. Burton took one look at the place and fished sandwiches and flask out of the boot. This was not a place where you went around to the kitchen and hoped for a welcome, Henry thought. One of the other cars still had a chauffeur in residence. He was reading a newspaper and Henry guessed that he and Burton would at least become acquainted while he and Mickey were inside.

In the vast hallway, marble-floored and very chilly, they were greeted by a woman in a formal black dress who checked their names in her book. Two young women sat on a bench seat and one rose when Henry came in. 'Inspector Johnstone,' she said and Henry recognized her as Violet Everson, the girl he had glimpsed on the stairs at the Everson residence the day before.

'Miss Everson?' He shook the gloved hand and looked curiously at the second young woman.

'This is Pat, Pat Moran. She is . . . She was Faun's older sister.'

Pat Moran had dark-brown hair caught up in a knot in the nape of her neck. Her face was pretty but looked pinched and chilled and Henry was not sure if this was the frigid nature of the atrium or grief at what had happened to her sister.

'I asked Pat to drive up with me,' Violet said. 'I wanted to be here when you spoke to Mal, but I didn't really want to be on my own. Pat needs to know what is going on so she said she'd come along. You have to understand our parents don't know we are here. Pat's father would definitely not approve and mine would think it was none of my business. He has some funny, old-fashioned ideas about what girls should be involved in and what they shouldn't. Sometimes he is just too, too overprotective.'

'I believe you know my sister,' Henry hazarded.

'Cynthia, yes indeed I do. In fact we both do. She called me, I said we'd do what we could to arrange a meeting with Mal, so, here we all are.'

'And when your father finds out?' Mickey asked. 'I expect he will, you know.'

Violet Everson shrugged. 'Then he'll blow his top, like he always does. Don't worry, Sergeant, I'm used to it, and most of the time it's just a lot of noise. I want to know what happened that day. Faun is dead, and so is that other girl, whoever she was, and my brother got the blame and I don't think that's fair. Now, shall we go up, it's freezing down here. At least Mal's rooms are kept warm.'

Violet evidently knew the way and they trooped up the stairs after her. Pat Moran looked unhappy and Henry wondered if she was regretting her decision to come. Violet's father might merely blow his top and make a lot of noise, but Caius Moran was known to be a man who disliked anyone going against his will. As though reading his thoughts, she said, 'Don't worry, Inspector, I'm a married woman and don't live with my father any more. He can't even threaten to cut off my allowance now because as of last year I came into my mother's money and so I can now do what I like. Poor Faun would have had five more years before she could say the same.'

'I see,' Henry said. He wondered if he should say more but

Violet was already knocking on a door and then opening it. The wall of warm air was welcome and a little overwhelming after the chill of the entranceway, the stairs and the corridor. These places must be hell to heat in winter, Henry thought. He wondered how many layers the woman in the formal black dress needed if she was to remain in her post all day, though her manner had been as icy as her surroundings so maybe she didn't notice.

Mal Everson sat in an armchair by the window and at first looked bewildered when everyone came in and Henry wondered if he had actually been expecting them or not. Then the young man's expression cleared a little and he got up to greet his sister with a hug and, perhaps surprisingly, welcomed Pat with a kiss on the cheek. There was, Henry calculated, a five- or six-year age gap between Pat and Violet. He guessed that Violet was perhaps twenty, and that Pat was probably twenty-five, that being a common enough age at which bequests reverted from trust status. Faun Moran had been not quite twenty when she died. It seemed that the young people from both families, or the sisters at least, had been drawn together by common grief and common anger.

Mal Everson had two rooms, a bedroom and this small sitting room. A spirit kettle was boiling and Pat, clearly familiar with the establishment, fetched the tea caddy and pot from the cupboard and set about preparing refreshments. Violet settled her brother back in the chair, the excitement of greeting everyone seeming to have worn him out. Malcolm Everson was pale and thin, his face drawn and his frame bony. His clothes seemed to hang from his narrow shoulders, like those on a scarecrow. Looking into his eyes, Henry was reminded of young men he had seen in battle, who had lost all sense of where they were and how they got there. Mal reminded Henry of himself.

Henry drew up a chair opposite Malcolm's and studied the young man thoughtfully. He was aware of Mickey hovering, no doubt making certain that his boss did not say anything too harsh. Henry knew that he was not always the most tactful or careful of men, but the look in Everson's eyes established a kind of kinship, because Henry recognized what it meant.

The deep and enduring sense of shock and dissociation and loss of self.

'Tell me about that day,' Henry said. 'What you remember. What do you think happened?'

'They say it wasn't Faun. How can it not be Faun? Faun was in my car. I crashed my car, I . . . killed . . . her. They tell me I had been drinking. Heavily, but I don't remember that. Truthfully I don't remember much.'

Mickey grabbed another chair and set it down close to Henry's. 'What do you remember about that day, not about the crash, but earlier than that? We've been told you arrived at the Belmonts' house at about eleven o'clock in the morning?'

'We arrived together,' Pat said unexpectedly. 'We had driven up together. I knew Faun was going to be at the party and I hadn't seen her in a while, so when Mal said he was going up on the Saturday, I asked if I could tag along. Since Faun and Father fell out she'd not been home, though she'd come to stay with me a time or two when she ran short of money. Our father had cut off her allowance when she refused to "behave" as he put it, But what with one thing and another I'd not seen much of her lately.'

'Your father had cut off her allowance, or threatened to, so—'

'So what was she living on?' Pat said flatly. 'Oh dear, you may well ask. I helped out where I could, and she was sharing a place in London with two other girls, and Frank, that's our brother, had done his best to persuade our father to at least pay her rent and give her a *small* allowance. Frank made him realize just how bad it would look if she ran up huge debts. But Faun would not have been able to manage just on that.' She looked away, clearly embarrassed.

Henry was about to press further but Mickey interrupted again and, looking at Mal, Henry realized that he was correct to do so. Mal Everson would not stand much questioning and already he was exhausted and becoming distressed. Some men, Henry thought, were just more fragile than others and that was no fault of theirs. All men had their breaking point and it seemed Mal Everson had met with his when his car had come off the road and crashed down the hill.

'So you arrived at about eleven,' Mickey said gently. 'Tell me all you can. What happened after that?'

'There was a buffet set out so we had a late breakfast or early lunch. I had one champagne cocktail. To be truthful I'm not that keen. I had coffee and I think, I think I ate eggs, perhaps some toast.' He looked at Pat for confirmation and the woman nodded.

'Not everyone was up – the party had apparently gone on till about four in the morning. Friday night there was a theme, Ancient Rome or some such, and some guests hadn't gone to bed until the servants were starting their day. I suppose people started drifting down around one and others had lunch in their rooms.'

'And you saw Faun, when?'

'Oh, I asked one of the maids to tell her we'd arrived,' Pat said, 'and she came down, still in her dressing gown while we were eating.'

Pat paused, a faint smile on her lips. 'She was pleased to see us,' she said. 'She hugged me and gave Mal a kiss on the cheek and then we sat and ate and drank coffee for an hour and then when she went up to get dressed I went up and chatted to her while she got ready. She was happy,' Pat added, before they could ask.

'She seemed . . . excited,' Mal Everson said.

'Excited? About anything in particular?'

Malcolm Everson and Pat exchanged a look as though each was trying to remember. Then Mal slumped back in his chair. 'Just excited, happy. I don't even remember what we talked about.'

Henry did not press him. He could get the gist of the conversation from Pat later on. Instead he said, 'And after that, what did you do?'

'I remember going on to the terrace to smoke a cigarette. I sat on the steps and looked out over the lawn and I remember having a conversation with someone, with two or three people maybe, but I couldn't tell you what about and I'm not even sure with who. It's all confused, who I spoke to then, who I talked to later in the afternoon. It's all kind of blurred and when I try and take hold of it, the harder I try the more confused it becomes and I know that's not very useful to you and I know you must think it's very convenient for me but it happens to be the truth.'

Violet came over and perched on the windowsill and took her brother's hand. She glanced anxiously at Henry as though warning him off. 'You told me that when you got in the car you felt ill,' she said.

Slowly, Malcolm Everson nodded. 'I truly don't believe I'd had much to drink,' he said. 'I drank the champagne cocktail, more to be polite than anything, and then I think I had a couple of whiskey and sodas in the afternoon. The butler, I think, brought me one, and I think Faun gave me the other.'

'We've asked around,' Violet said, 'and as near as we can find out Mal is remembering right. He hadn't been drinking heavily, three drinks since about eleven o'clock that morning, the last about an hour before they went out, or maybe a little less than an hour. But he wasn't drunk, no matter what everyone assumed.'

'So you felt ill.' Mickey returned to what had also seemed to Henry to be the important factor. 'Can you tell us all you can remember after Miss Moran suggested you go for a drive?'

Malcolm Everson closed his eyes and leaned back. His sister gripped his hand hard and Pat Moran took the other one. These three were evidently close, Henry thought, and also clearly dissatisfied with the official verdict.

'She gave me a Scotch and soda and said how about going for a spin. I said that I'd be happy to take her and where did she want to go. She told me she didn't care, she just wanted to get out and about for a bit, that she had something to tell me and because we've been friends for such a long time she wanted me to be the first to know.

'I remember laughing at that because although we had known each other for a long time it's not like we'd been particular friends. I liked her but we were just part of the same crowd. She was always like the little sister, you know. Pat and Frank and I were always closer, I suppose, because we're that bit closer in age. But she seemed so happy that I thought I'd humour her, I do kind of remember that. I finished my drink while she got herself ready and I remember speaking to someone in the hall and Faun was dancing around me – that girl never walked anywhere.' His smile was sad, his eyes still closed as though it was easier to remember that way.

'Do you remember collecting the car?'

'Not really. I'd parked in the stable yard. I think we went out the front way and I vaguely recall speaking to someone on the way out. Faun . . . I think Faun had mislaid her coat and thought it might be hanging in the hall. It can get cold in the car. Next thing I really do remember was being out on the road and feeling so sick. Dizzy, hazy, you know. Faun said there was a farm gate, at least I think that's what she said. She said to pull over and she would drive. She joked I must have had too much to drink but I know I hadn't. Violet and Pat know. They've asked everybody that was there, everybody that could know anything and everybody knows I don't drink much.'

'And do you remember pulling over? We drove that road a few days ago, from what we noticed there were not many spots where you could have pulled the car in.'

Mal Everson screwed up his eyes as though that might help and then shook his head. 'I've tried, believe me I have tried. The last thing I remember clearly is feeling ill and Faun saying that we should pull over so she could drive and then there is nothing. It's like there's a blank space in my brain and I cannot, I cannot remember.'

'The doctors say he's blocking things out,' Violet said coldly.

'You don't believe that?' Henry asked.

'No. I don't. I believe something happened. What if she put something in his drink? What if someone else did?'

· The same thought had crossed Henry's mind. He glanced at Pat, wondering if Faun's sister had a similar perspective on the matter or if she was less sympathetic of Malcolm Everson's position, but Pat nodded. 'Malcolm is right. My sister did seem happy, she did seem excited, and she said she'd have some news for me later. I assumed she'd just fallen in love again. Faun was always falling in love and falling out again just as quickly. And I've known Mal since we were all children, and I know he doesn't drink to excess. He'd never drive if he had more than say three drinks. He's not like some, convinced that the more alcohol they imbibe the better drivers they become.'

Henry looked keenly at Malcolm Everson. The young man was even paler, his skin pasty and grey, and a sheen of sweat had broken out on his forehead. Despite this, he looked cold. 'What's the first thing you remember afterwards?' he asked.

'Waking up in hospital, feeling confused and in pain and not knowing what had happened. At some time, I don't know how much later, someone told me Faun was dead, that we had crashed off the road and I think I must have gone a little mad for a time. I think I must still be a little mad. They brought me here, and here I've stayed ever since.'

'I think he's had enough, Inspector,' Violet said.

Henry nodded. 'There is just one more thing. Did you intend to stop for a picnic? Can you remember anything being said about that?'

Malcolm Everson looked surprised and shook his head, but then he nodded slowly. 'She said it might be fun, that we could talk, and there was a picnic basket in the car. I assumed she must have packed it and . . . I just don't remember her taking it to the car. Just her saying that there was a picnic basket in the car.'

They had brought the suitcase and Gladstone bag and when they had entered the room Mickey had parked them by the door. He fetched them now and set them down on the floor at Malcolm Everson's feet. 'Do you remember these bags also being in the car?'

Malcolm Everson's face was a picture of disbelief and confusion. 'Why would they be in the car?'

'Do you recognize the bags?' The question was put to all three of the young people.

'The bag is mine,' Malcolm said. 'We were only staying one night, so I didn't bring a lot. But I had unpacked my bag and put it in the bottom of the wardrobe. I don't know why it was there.'

'I don't recognize the other one,' Pat said. 'I don't think it was Faun's.'

'Both bags were found at the scene, along with the items that were inside them. They were presumably gathered up by those at the scene and put back in the car when it was removed. Since then both car and its contents have been left in a barn on the estate and no one seems to have looked at them until we came along. Perhaps you could look inside and tell me if you recognize anything.'

Mal Everson recognized shirts and the cufflinks. The clothes were his own, ones he had packed for the weekend.

'But I'd swear these are not Faun's,' Pat said. 'For one thing she rarely wore slacks, and for another the quality is poor. I think too that the waist is larger. I doubt these would have fitted Faun.' She intercepted the glance between Henry and Mickey. 'What?'

'When she was left on the beach, the clothes she wore were not her own,' Henry told her. 'But I'd be grateful if that goes no further than this room.'

'Do you think these clothes belong to the poor dead woman in the car?' Violet asked.

'We think that's possible. We also found a compact, a cheap little brass thing,' Mickey said. 'Though,' he added, the thought just occurring to him, 'if the compact was hers then that does not fit with the quality of clothing Faun was wearing when she was left on the beach.'

'Faun had a silver compact. I suppose she could have sold it, but I think that's unlikely. Our mother gave it to her for her fifteenth birthday, so it was very precious. My mother died a few months later and Faun . . . Well, Faun was never the same again.'

They left very soon after. They had moved Malcolm to a chair close to the fire, covered him with a blanket and he had instantly fallen asleep.

Once outside Pat Moran eyed the suitcase warily as though it might bite. 'There is a tearoom down the road in the next village, and I don't know about anybody else, but I'm hungry. And I also think, gentlemen, that we have more to talk about.'

Henry readily agreed and they followed Pat Moran's car as she and Violet drove back to the village.

'This is a pretty pickle,' Mickey observed. 'But it seems in this the younger members of the family have more sense than their elders and more of a sense of justice too.'

'And it is through them that we shall reach the truth, I think,' Henry agreed. 'But Mickey, I have the strangest feeling that this truth is going to be one that no one will welcome. There will be nothing clean and simple about it.'

The tearoom was picturesque, Henry supposed. He noted Mickey looking around with satisfaction. Sometimes his sergeant had a disturbing liking for twee. China teapots decorated high shelves alongside rose-patterned plates and the walls were covered with pictures by local artists, or so the signage told him. He assumed that in the summer season this place would be very busy, but at this time of year, still cold and chill, there were only a handful of people. They were shown to a table for six in the corner and a neatly dressed waitress took their order. Henry was aware that she looked askance at these two impeccably dressed women accompanied by two not so impeccably dressed older males and a young male in the uniform of the police driver (Constable Burton having been invited in for warmth and refreshments) and wondered what conclusion she was drawing.

'I'll be mother, shall I?' Pat Moran said. She had shed her winter coat and beneath it she was wearing a beautifully tailored suit in blue wool with a crisp, cream, silk blouse. She was a very self-possessed young woman, Henry thought, now mistress of her own household and with two children, apparently. Both these women, Pat and Violet, would have been at home in Cynthia's company and that set him somewhat at his ease.

Constable Burton looked less so, he was clearly out of his depth and not quite sure whether he should be speaking or sitting in a corner like a child, there to be seen and not heard.

Afternoon tea distributed, Pat said, 'So, do you think he was drugged? Did she slip him a Mickey Finn or something?'

'It does seem possible,' Henry agreed. 'Of course, the doctors could also be right and he is blocking much of this out. I don't mean to suggest that he is doing so deliberately, but sometimes the mind cannot cope and so chooses to forget.'

Violet was watching him cautiously and now said, 'I have heard of such things happening to those who have been in the war, but the circumstances are different here.'

'Not so different,' Henry assured her. 'When something happens that cannot be dealt with, sometimes the mind simply puts it aside until it can and it could be that your brother will remember more, given time. But now we do not have time and so we must work without his memory and focus simply on the evidence that we have.'

Violet nodded, picked up a fork and prodded at her cake. 'You may have gathered that our families would not approve of our continuing friendship, and certainly would not approve of the fact that we were complicit in your visit to Mal.'

'We had gathered that,' Mickey told her. 'And you may be sure we are grateful.'

'We spoke of this between ourselves and decided what we really needed was to know the truth,' Pat told him. 'We may not like the truth when we see it, but at least we will know what happened. And there is more to my sister's death than originally met the eye. I was certain of that from the beginning, and so was Vi. We know our siblings, their weaknesses included. I know that Faun was by all ways of accounting wild, ill-disciplined and extremely foolish. She was also loving and so very alive. Alive in ways I have never been able to be. I cared deeply about my little sister and I continue to care even though she is now dead. Twice dead. That is what hurts so much. We had just come to terms with our loss when suddenly we are to lose her all over again. It is beyond bearing, Inspector, I'm sure you can see that. So the truth must out, however painful it is, however disagreeable it might be to our fathers.'

'Are you not worried about their anger?' Mickey asked.

'Violet has more to lose than I do, but Violet will come into her own money in a year's time and there is nothing her father can do about that. As for me, I am already an independent woman, married and no longer answerable to my father. As it happens, my husband agrees with my actions. He hopes that there will be no scandal attached, of course, but he can hardly be held responsible even if there is. And as a man of independent means, he does not have to listen to anyone, even if they do drag his wife's family through the mire. Sometimes there are advantages to marrying an arrogant man.' She said this last with a small smile and fondness in her voice that Henry found intriguing.

'And is your older brother in agreement?' Mickey asked Violet Everson.

She shrugged. 'My father and my brother Ford and I rarely see eye to eye on anything much. My father has taken all steps to avoid the issue and he will be away from home until all of this trouble has died down. My brother thinks I should keep out of things that don't concern me, both as his sister and as a woman, which means just about anything of importance. I don't mean to give the impression that he's a bad sort, only that he's a little traditional when it comes to the place of women. But I no longer care what Ford thinks, or my father for that matter. As Pat says, a year from now, none of it will matter. I will be able to do as I please and if that means that this year will be difficult, so be it. I am not a woman to be ruled by the menfolk in my family, Sergeant Hitchens, you may be sure of that.'

Mickey nodded thoughtfully. Henry, glancing at Constable Burton, saw that the young man looked stunned, sitting open-mouthed, staring at these two young viragos. 'Drink your tea, Constable,' Henry said sternly. Constable Burton closed his mouth and lifted his cup obediently to his lips. His gaze, however, never left Violet.

'So,' Henry said, 'we have several considerations here. The identity of the young woman in the car, where Miss Faun Moran has been for these last six months, and who caused the deaths of both. These matters are all undoubtedly interlinked, we cannot examine them in isolation.'

'The young woman now buried in the family crypt,' Mickey said, 'that I'm told your father now wants exhumed . . . did you see the body before burial?'

Pat Moran nodded. 'I demanded to. I couldn't believe that Faun was gone. My father didn't want me to see her. He said it would be too upsetting. In fact, my father refused to see the body; he said he wanted to remember his child as she had been in life, not after such a god-awful death. So I went to the undertakers, and I stamped my feet, I'm afraid, and behaved like a complete brat until the poor man gave in. I couldn't believe it, and I needed to say a proper goodbye, you understand?'

'And you are certain that it was Faun?'

For the first time Pat looked uncomfortable and she found it hard to meet Mickey's eyes. 'For once my father was probably right,' she said. 'It would have been better not to have seen. She was burnt, and her face was . . . broken. There is no other word for it. My beautiful little sister, all shattered and unrecognizable. I looked quickly and then, I'm afraid, I turned away.'

'But you felt certain it was her? The identification was largely dependent on the fact that she was seen getting into Mr Everson's car,' Mickey pressed.

'Yes. She was wearing pieces of my sister's jewellery. Besides, what reason was there to doubt it at the time? Several people knew she was going for a drive with Mal. It was his car found crashed, he was found close by badly injured, she was in the car burnt and the car was burnt. Who else could it have been? At least that was the way we thought when it happened. And now . . . now we know that it was some other poor unfortunate. But my sister is still dead. What is going on here, Inspector? Why did the original investigation not realize this body was not my sister's?'

'Because no one was looking for anything else,' Henry said coldly. 'What were deemed to be the facts were presented and no one looked further. From what I can gather the families wanted the matter cleared up very quickly and as quietly and simply as possible. But from those who viewed the crime scene, and I have no doubt now that it was a *crime* scene, we are now also coming to the belief that the fire was set after the crash, rapidly and efficiently. Undoubtedly the car would have been consumed and the body with it had it not been for strange chance that brought others on to the scene. Others who put the fire out and preserved what we now realize was evidence of a crime.'

'Tell us,' Violet demanded. 'What was seen?'

Henry looked at the now very discomfited Constable Burton, who had suddenly realized that this was his payment for tea and cake. That he must tell these two women what he had

witnessed on the day and just after and what he had been told
by Farmer Carter and his son-in-law. With a little prompting
from Mickey he began his story. Questions from the two
women filled out what he forgot to say. A half hour later they
were both much better informed and even more deeply
shocked.

'So if I have this right,' Violet said, 'it is likely that
my brother was drugged, that he did not drive the car,
that perhaps Faun – and I am sorry to say this out loud, my
dear' – this to Pat – 'perhaps drove the car and was in some
way complicit in the disposal of this young woman's body.
I'm assuming she was not alive when the fire was set?'

'We must hope not,' Mickey said.

'Indeed, the alternative is too terrible to contemplate. This
whole business is too terrible to contemplate.' Violet reached
across the table and took Pat's hand. 'What did she get herself
into?'

'No,' Pat said firmly. 'What did someone else get her into?
Faun would never willingly injure any other person, of that
I'm certain. She must have been pressured, blackmailed
possibly. Someone made her do this.'

'And yet you say she seemed happy at the party. That there
was no sign of anxiety. That she had news for you,' Henry
reminded her.

Pat scowled at him and then her expression softened and
she nodded. 'She did. She was the happiest I have seen her
in quite some time.'

'And you have no sense of what this news might have been
about?'

'As I said before, I assumed it was about some man or other.
It usually was. Faun had very little in terms of common sense
when it came to men. I hoped she would acquire some given
time and the truth is most of us were stupid about some man
or other when we were young. It is as well most of us are not
punished for the indiscretions of when we are eighteen or
nineteen or we would all be in trouble.'

'Your sister was intelligent. Would she not have realized
that she was getting into something far too deeply?'

'I think,' Mickey said, 'that she was also something of a

romantic? And that perhaps the death of your mother hit her particularly badly, am I right?'

'I'm afraid you are, on both counts,' Pat admitted. She poured herself more tea and sat thinking for a moment or two and then she said, 'I challenged her, asked her if her news was about a man and she said that she had found someone special. But she was afraid that I might not approve. I asked her immediately if that meant that he was a married man and she said that it was nothing like that, but that this was not her usual type and so I might find it strange. Then I'm afraid we were interrupted by someone knocking on the door and it was clear that Faun was looking for an excuse not to say anything more and we both came downstairs again.'

'Not her usual type of man?' Mickey asked.

'I may be completely wrong but I got the impression that he was older. That she had fallen for an older man. But I know nothing. If I did, I'd tell you. What is there to lose now?'

The waitress appeared and asked if they required any more tea and no one spoke much until she had brought a fresh teapot and more hot water. Then Henry asked, 'Were you actually invited to the house party? Only you weren't on the list we were given.'

'As a matter of fact I was. I probably still have the invitation somewhere.'

'Why would Mrs Belmont leave you off the list she gave to us?'

Pat shrugged. 'Probably because the invite came from Eliza. Mrs B doesn't know the half of what goes on under her roof and she wasn't even in residence that weekend. I wasn't gate-crashing, but nobody would have cared if I had been.'

'From what we've heard that happens a lot at house parties.'

Violet laughed. 'The truth is people don't always realize they're having a house party until we all turn up.' She sobered. 'But I imagine all of that's going to change now with all the business of the stock market crash and Wall Street. Even late last year, well, it all felt so different, you know? People pulling in their horns and cutting back and just not being quite as willing to . . . to entertain, I suppose. I mean, we don't exactly move in the rarefied circles of the Mitfords and the Ponsonbys. We might occasionally run with the same crowd but what the world refers to as the Bright Young Things are in a different league altogether.'

She sounded, Henry thought, slightly dismissive.

'So no bath and bottle parties for you?' Mickey asked.

Violet laughed at that. 'All the world and his wife went to that event, or at least you'd think so from the way people talk. "Too, too sick-making to be left out",' she mimicked and then shook her head disparagingly. 'My allowance doesn't quite run to that many changes of bathing suit. My folks are well off, by any measure, but not out of the top drawer. My mother was from minor nobility and so that opens doors but even so . . .'

'What about Faun?' Henry asked Pat.

'Oh, doors opened anyway for Faun,' she said softly. 'Even those that really should have stayed closed. For her own sake.'

'What do you mean by that?'

Pat hesitated as though wondering what she should say. If she should say anything. Then she shrugged. 'She boasted that her friends in London took her to the Gargoyle Club and . . . that she danced the evening away at the Savoy and then went on to these little underground places where you had to *know someone*, as she put it, before they allowed you in. She mentioned gambling and even a boxing match on one occasion, but when I tried to press her she just clammed up and told me I was being a bore. I told her she was far too young, warned her of the scandal if it came out. What if there was a police raid? But even though she was far too young to be legal, she was always in the company of far older associates.

'In many ways, Faun was a little fool,' Pat said. 'But I loved her, fool or not. And the trouble was she had as much sense of caution as a cat leaping between roofs. She thought just because she found one thing easy that everything else would be too.'

'What did she find easy?' Mickey asked.

'Getting her own way, attracting men, even if they were the wrong sort of man. Getting people to like her. I mean, that was effortless.' She sat back, looking suddenly defeated. 'I suppose when we're very young we all feel we know about the world and as we get older we all realize we know nothing. The sad thing is my sister didn't have a chance to comprehend all the things she didn't know.'

'And she never mentioned names?'

Pat sighed. 'She mentioned names. She dropped names, if you will. I was never certain if there was any truth to the matter of it or if she was just trying to impress me.'

'And the names?' Mickey pressed gently.

'Best tell them, Pat,' Violet urged her. 'We agreed, remember. We need the truth, no matter how ghastly it might be.'

Pat nodded reluctantly. She withdrew a small aide memoire from her purse and wrote three names down. Folded the paper and pushed it across the table towards Henry. 'I may be totally wrong,' she said softly, 'but I suspect . . . I suspect the last name on that list is the man Faun believed herself to be involved with. To be in love with.'

Henry placed his fingertips on the paper but did not open it. This, he sensed, was a potential breaking point in the relationship they had built with these two young women. I'll go this far, Pat was telling him, but don't press me. I've already said more to you than I have to anyone else. He could feel Mickey's gaze resting on him, willing him to know when to give the matter his best and leave it alone.

'You said you believed her to be involved with the last name on the list,' Henry said.

'A fantasy,' Pat said simply. 'What would a man like that want with a slip of a girl like my sister? It's too absurd.'

A few minutes later Henry stood watching the two young women drive away. They had decided, as it was already dark, to call on friends where they would be assured of hospitality for the night and drive home the following day. Constable Burton and Mickey now awaited him in the car. It was strange, he thought, where people drew their line in the sand. He wondered about Pat; had she perhaps fancied herself in love with this same man and been knocked back? Was that why she could not conceive of her sister being involved with him?

'So, who do we have on that slip of paper?' Mickey asked as Henry got into the car.

'Two names that I find predictable. Evan Klein runs with the Connaughts and their set. He's louche, effeminate, and a writer of sorts, and Cecil Beaton likes to take his picture, I believe. But there's not a young woman of quality whose name hasn't been associated at some point or other. The second is Martyn Cairns, an intellectual—'

'And close to Mosley, from what I've heard. Something of a fascist. Doesn't he give public lectures? I have a memory of disturbances after one and the constables having to restore order.'

'It would not surprise me. The third name, however, is interesting. Benjamin Caxton, decorated war hero, son of a peer of the realm. Has fingers in a dozen political pies and as many business ones. I believe Cynthia's Albert may have had some dealings with him.'

'Severely injured during the war. Lost an eye and was badly burned.' Mickey nodded. 'I have seen him in the newspapers.'

'Not a man you'd associate with a flighty child,' Henry said.

TEN

They had returned to London on the Monday morning and mid-afternoon found Henry back at his flat contemplating a lonely few hours until it was time to go to bed. He was still finding it hard to settle and, unusually for him, hard to be alone. Mickey had invited him back but Henry had declined. Monday evenings were one of the few times that Mickey and Belle could actually claim as their own, when the theatre was dark and she was not performing. He knew they treasured the time that they could spend together and he would not willingly have intruded upon that even though he knew that he would have been welcome.

He telephoned Cynthia, eager for the sound of a familiar voice and for ordinary news and for a while they talked about random things.

She joked that Henry Johnstone's return from retirement in order to take on this new and mysterious case shared billing on the front page with Pope Pius XI's proclamations about the sinfulness of co-educational schools.

'Are you coping with this, Henry?' she asked him.

'So far I am. I confess I'm still finding it hard work, just being on my feet all day and thinking what I must ask people, what questions come next. I think if Mickey wasn't present I would struggle but Mickey knows how I work, how I think, what needs to be done and that helps to keep me moving in the right direction.'

'It will take time, Henry. Be patient with yourself.'

Henry smiled. 'Patience was never one of my virtues,' he confessed.

'Cynthia, have you ever had dealings with a Mr Benjamin Caxton? His name has come up and I had this vague memory that Albert did business with him at one time.'

'On one occasion, yes. But he is not a man we have cultivated. He does not have the best of reputations for honesty,
Henry, and he is very much the politician these days. I believe
his business affairs have been handed over for others to
manage. It was his father that we had more connection with.
Cyril Caxton was a nice man and Albert's father and he were
great friends at one time.'

'And did something happen to end that friendship?'

'No, I don't believe so. I think it was simply that neither
was as active in business. Both had retired and Cyril retreated
to the countryside. He took a great interest in hunting
and local politics and I believe in fishing. Essentially he
retired and became an English gentleman in habit as well as
in family name. Albert's father, as you know, took to travelling, so I don't think there was any great falling out, more a
simple drift apart.'

'But you've had no real dealings with the son.'

He could sense Cynthia thinking about this, carefully
considering her response. 'You know that Ben was wounded,
badly so. He barely made it home with his life. There is no
doubting his courage.'

'But?'

'But he's a predator, Henry.'

'Predator? What exactly do you mean?'

'I think you know what I mean. As women gain experience,
they learn to recognize the type. Men too, but men seem to
idolise them. Women will either run like hell or fall for the
charisma.' She paused, as though thinking. 'You remember
that friend of our father's? Another doctor, a man called Rice.'

'All too well.'

'He's like that, but with the money and power and
reputation to support his baser instincts and give them outlet.
And, like Rice, I believe Benjamin Caxton has a fondness for
widows. Preferably wealthy, older widows.'

'But Rice wasn't averse to young girls either, from what I
remember.'

'Don't remind me. The memory is still disgusting and
distasteful.'

Rice, Henry remembered, had been the one person among

their father's old associates to offer them any kind of assistance after his death. *Come and stay with me, he'd said, his voice kind and concerned, his hand reaching for Cynthia's. It would be perfectly proper, as you know my dear sister lives with me and so you would not be alone in the house.*

I have my brother to look after.

Of course. And he will be most welcome until we can make some other arrangements. A charity scholarship perhaps, or an apprenticeship. You can't possibly manage alone.

At the time Henry had not fully understood his sister's tight-lipped anger as she had declined. Cynthia had not been worldly or experienced enough to comprehend exactly what he wanted but she knew enough to be wary. Rice was enough like their father and had been close enough to him that she knew his type and had no wish to jump from the frying pan into the fire. And as it happened, she and Henry had managed very well alone, with only the slightest of assistance from anybody else.

'Rice was powerful within our own small community,' Henry mused. 'Wealthy too, compared to many.'

'Several bequests from sick, grateful patients I seem to remember. As I said, he was fond of widows. I remember hearing our father laughing over one poor woman who had given him gifts and money and you can guess what else and then had been cast aside once he'd bled her dry. Why are you asking about him? I mean not about Dr Rice, but about Ben Caxton?'

'Because it's rumoured, and only rumoured, that he took an interest in young Faun Moran. And that she fancied herself in love with him.'

'Well, if that's true it is not a good thing to have happened. In fact, it is a vile thing to have happened. What could a young thing like Faun Moran know about dealing with a phony like Caxton? She might have fancied herself in love, she might even have fancied that the feelings were returned, but no, Henry, the man is a predator, an amoral degenerate.'

'Harsh words.'

'And I will not take them back, Henry. If you are dealing with this man then be careful.'

'I think he's hardly as dangerous as others I've had unfortunate dealings with lately.'

'While it's true he might not attack you from behind and break your shoulder, I put very little else past him. And before you ask, no, I've no evidence for that. He's just not a man I like, or am comfortable being close to, or who I believe for one instant is anything like his public face.'

'I will be careful,' Henry promised her.

'Don't just say the words, Henry – mean them. I think you might be interested in his manservant, or friend, or whatever you want to call him. He employs a man called Victor Mullins and, while I had no reason to call him to mind before, of course, it now seems to me that Victor Mullins would be a good match for the man on the beach. He's a big man, well over six feet tall and built like an oak door. Old Mr Caxton employed him as a general factotum and the son has done the same.'

'And what do you know about this Victor Mullins?'

'Not a great deal. He drives for the Caxtons. Old Mr Caxton used a wheelchair for the last few years of his life and I think Mr Mullins helped with that, and with lifting and general assistance. But it was more than that. I called him a factotum and I think that is an accurate description. I believe he was a boxer at one time, and of course he served in the Great War and it may have been there that he met Ben, but I can't be sure.'

It was food for thought. The conversation moved to other things, to the children and to Albert and to the weather down in Bournemouth which looked to be improving.

When he had asked Cynthia about Ben Caxton he had been looking for just a little background information, a generalized opinion of the man and his status. But it struck him that it was very unusual for Cynthia to be so vehement in her disapproval of anyone. He wondered what this Caxton had done to upset her so much. Suddenly Caxton had gone from a name written on a slip of paper to a real possibility in terms of the investigation and the direction it might take next.

Evening brought news – unexpected news. A telephone call from the Central Office told Henry that Caius Moran had finally agreed to speak with them. They were to take the train to Brighton and Moran had arranged for a car to collect them from the station and bring them to his estate on the South Downs. A message had been sent to Sergeant Hitchens and they would meet at the railway station at ten a.m. the following morning.

His colleague at Central Office warned him that Moran seemed far more interested in how quickly the police could arrange for the body of the young woman to be exhumed and out of the family grave she currently occupied than about helping with their enquiry, but at this point, Henry considered, anything that gave them access to Caius Moran was useful and he would settle for that.

ELEVEN

Faun, December

S ometimes he allows me to go downstairs to his study.
Sometimes to have a bath. I welcome those occasions so
much that I take care to behave – so that I am seen to
deserve them.

*Downstairs, it is safe. Up in that little room it is not. Oh,
Pat, he comes to me at night, sometimes alone but often with
that bastard friend of his. And he hurts me so. He takes pleasure
in my pain. He is never satisfied unless he leaves me in tears
and in pain.*

But I will not think of that now.

*He lets me go downstairs for a little while. I try to be inter-
ested in what he is doing. I try to make him like me, to behave
towards me as he used to do. When he was kind and told me
that he loved me. That we would be married. That all changed
once he brought me here after the party.*

*Pat, to think I would once have welcomed that. I had such
romantic notions. But that was just so much bunkum. He told
me what he knew I would want to hear and I just lapped
it up.*

*He was messing with that microscope of his. He showed it
to me once, when he was still treating me like a human being.
He showed it to me and I confess I was not much interested.
There was too much of the schoolroom about it and I had
endured enough of the schoolroom. But this time I asked him
to show me. I fawned upon him and I flattered and though I
don't know if he was taken in, he showed me the slides he
had made with blood and hair and cells taken from his cheeks,
or so he said. And I told him how clever he was and how
wonderful it all seemed. And while he was turned momentarily
away I slipped one of his unused slides into my pocket.*

I think I imagined using it as a weapon. I had imagined

how brave I could be, cutting at his face or his remaining eye,
but what good would that do me? He locks the door to the
hidden stair each and every time we pass through. If I could
leave my room I could not get further than the bottom of the
staircase and no one would hear me, I'm sure of that, no
matter how hard I banged upon the door or how loudly I
should scream. The staircase sounds like a dead room.

But I had one little victory. I managed to snatch a glimpse
of a newspaper and I saw the date. I know now that today is
the fifteenth of December. I know when I came here – so long
ago. Oh, God, Pat, so long ago – and I can use my little scrap
of glass to mark the floor beneath my bed as each day passes.

Though what good that's going to do me I can't say.

Tuesday 14 January

The journey down had been uneventful. The car collected them
and delivered them to the Moran estate. The house was a
strangely castellated affair that would not have looked out of
place on a Hollywood film set, Mickey thought. It had been
created to look antique but apparently had been built only in
the last ten years. 'Someone knows how to spend money,'
Mickey commented.

The house was raised above the surrounding formal gardens
and the entranceway designed to be imposing. Doors that must
be ten feet high, Mickey reckoned, and almost as broad, heavy
and panelled and carved with grotesque masks. They were
admitted to a surprisingly small, square hallway, stairs rising
up ahead, doors to either side. The butler led them up the
stairs and to the right and into a major reception room with
windows all along one wall giving a view out on to the Downs.

The butler left them and Henry predictably wandered over
to the fire while Mickey went to look out of the windows. The
view was spectacular, the day was clear and Mickey could
glimpse the sea in the distance. Caius Moran did not keep
them waiting for long and he was not alone; with him was a
man he introduced as his lawyer, Mr Merrifield. Moran waved
them into seats in a corner of the room away from the fire.

Merrifield sat down, but Moran, obviously agitated, paced or
stood and threw his arms about like, Mickey thought, some
ham tragedian. Mickey had expected a larger man but Moran
was quite small, though stockily built and Mickey was
reminded of a bull terrier but without the personality.

'How did this happen?' Moran demanded. 'Your people told
me that my daughter was dead, and now it seems she was not,
that the corpse now residing in our family vault has nothing
to do with me or mine. And my daughter is *now* unequivocally
dead, I suppose there is no mistake this time.'

Moran had ignored Mickey and so he decided he would
remain silent for the moment. He recognized his boss's
expression, the cold, grey, river pebble eyes and stiffened
jaw and knew that Henry had taken an instant disliking to
their host. The last time Henry had taken a dislike to someone
it had not ended well, Mickey reminded himself. His boss
had taken trouble to demonstrate how powerful his right hook
could be. Mickey prepared himself for intervention should
things turn nasty, and in the meantime just sat back to watch
the show.

'You know full well there is no mistake,' Henry told him
coldly. 'And if you had permitted a post-mortem to have taken
place after the car crash I have no doubt the truth would have
been exposed at that point. We would all have known that the
young woman who died was not your child, that she was
someone else's daughter, someone else's loss.'

Mickey noticed that Merrifield shot an anxious look at his
client and that Moran's face was growing darker and redder
by the second.

'And if your people had carried out a proper investigation
in the first place, a post-mortem would not be necessary, this
business would have been resolved, and—'

'And the chances are your daughter would still be dead,'
Henry said. 'The young woman in the car was destined to
have been burnt, her body destroyed, the evidence that she
was not Miss Faun Moran destroyed. The intention was to
deceive. Whether the intention at that point was also to murder
your child, we do not yet know, but the intention undoubtedly
was to keep her from you and for you to believe her dead.'

Moran laughed harshly. 'What purpose would have been served by that?'

'That is another question I seek to answer.'

'Really. And you expect to succeed in that, do you? Excuse my lack of faith. Your original investigation was a mockery.'

'It was not my investigation. Had it been I do not doubt that the truth would have emerged. But the fact is, the *simple* fact is, that officers were called to what looked like an accident and nothing more suspicious than that. And the second fact is that pressure was brought to bear from your family and from Mr Everson's family to clear the matter up very quickly and quietly and discreetly. It was made known that no scandal was to be attached to the matter, that it was to be kept as much out of the newspapers as possible, and the whole matter brushed away as quickly and unobtrusively as could be managed.'

Mickey raised an eyebrow. They had absolutely no proof that this was the case though it was a solid enough assumption. Moran, however, seemed to believe that Henry was in possession of the facts. He halted in his pacing and turned to stare at Chief Inspector Johnstone. 'Take that tone with me and I'll report you to your superiors.'

Henry nodded. 'As you wish. But the fact is that your daughter is dead and that I am now leading the investigation into her death and I will get to the bottom of the matter. So I suggest that if you have information to give me you do so. And as to the poor young woman who has found her way into your family vault, I have arranged for the exhumation to take place, the body to be collected and taken away. A post-mortem will be carried out, so that whatever truth escaped the investigation last year will not escape us again.'

'I don't give a damn about her; I want to know what happened to my daughter.'

'I don't yet have the report from the surgeon, but the post-mortem will undoubtedly add to our knowledge and you will be informed. As to not caring what happened to this other poor young woman, Mr Moran, I have no doubt but that the fate of one is linked to the fate of the other, and the more we can discover about one the more you will discover about the other. I would also have you know that while *you* may not care, *I* care and my sergeant cares, as do all of the other officers that will be involved with this investigation. We will do all we can to give this girl a name and an identity and return her to her own people. Someone else is missing a child, a daughter. Somehow the death of this girl is linked to the death of your own child but one is not more important than the other. Both are tragic and both will command my full attention.'

Mickey felt like applauding but supposed that would not be the best response. Moran's face was beetroot now and Mickey wondered idly if he might explode and how much mess that might make. Moran made a point of looking at his wristwatch and then at his lawyer. He pointed at Henry, jabbing his finger, though wisely, Mickey thought, keeping his distance.

'You'll deal with Merrifield. Give him your documentation; he will facilitate the removal.'

'And what if I want other information?'

'Then you'll ask Merrifield,' Moran snapped. He turned on his heel and left the room. It was as though a storm cloud had departed and the sunlight come back through the windows.

Henry took out his notebook and removed a loose page which he handed to the lawyer. 'These are the details I need,' he said. 'Information that is relevant to the investigation. I will need to know how to contact you if I have other requirements. May I leave it to you to liaise with the undertakers? I'm sure it will please all involved if the removal of the body takes place quickly and quietly.'

Merrifield looked through the list and then nodded. 'If you could wait here for half an hour I can get the names and addresses you want,' he said. 'Then I'll arrange for the car to drive you back to Brighton. I imagine you will want to take the first available train back to London this afternoon.'

'Actually I think we will take the train to Bournemouth,' Henry said when Merrifield had gone. 'It's too late in the day to do anything else of use, we may as well stay the night at Cynthia's and travel back in the morning. The post-mortem report on Faun Moran should have arrived by the time we get there and, if Mr Merrifield can give us the information we require, we can interview the two young women that Miss Moran shared her lodgings with tomorrow afternoon.'

Merrifield was back within the half hour with the information Henry required and told them that the car was waiting.

'And that was something of a wasted trip, I think,' Mickey said. 'For all the help that Moran was. We could have spoken to his lawyer on the telephone. They didn't even offer us a cup of tea,' he added, aggrieved.

'I wanted to see the man himself,' Henry said. 'To make my own judgement about him.'

Mickey smiled; he didn't bother to ask what that judgement was.

Evening found them at Cynthia's, where the welcome was much warmer and Mickey, now fed and watered to his great satisfaction, extended his feet and legs towards the fire and folded his hands across his waistcoated belly. 'I don't think much of Mr Moran,' he told Cynthia. 'Though we like his daughter.'

'Pat is a good egg,' Cynthia agreed. 'And the elder brother is a nice enough man. He is less under his father's thumb now than he was, and I think he's improved as a result of that. So, did you find out anything useful? Could Mal tell you anything more?'

'He remembers very little,' Henry told her. 'He reminded me of young men suffering from shell-shock, that same detachment and inability to face their own memories. I don't think he's lying; I think he genuinely does not remember what took place. We have almost reached the conclusion that he was drugged in some way.'

'Drugged? Is that why he went off the road?'

'It's possible he wasn't even driving,' Mickey told her. 'He remembers feeling ill and that Faun Moran suggested that she take over the driving but he doesn't recall whether or not that happened.'

'It's also looking increasingly possible that *no one* was actually driving when the car went over the edge,' Henry added. 'It's increasingly possible that the entire incident was staged to make it look as though an accident had taken place. A local farmer heard the car as it rolled down the slope and came on the scene very rapidly. It was natural for him to assume he had also heard the car trying to brake before it went over the edge, but no skid marks were ever reported on the road, and while I believe that DI Shelton made only a cursory investigation of the scene, having met one of the young officers involved I am of the opinion that the local police would have reported skid marks on the road had they been there. The inference was that Malcolm Everson did not try to brake and he failed to make the bend and instead continued straight off the road and down into the valley. A very steep valley, I might add.'

'And the fire.' Mickey picked up the story. 'We were given to believe that the car had burst into flames when it hit the bottom and that the young woman had been consumed by the flames. We've no doubt that had things gone to plan that's exactly what would have happened, but for the intervention of the local farmer, Mr Carter and his son-in-law, who came to the rescue and put out the flames. They then sent for the doctor and the police. If they hadn't been there then things might have turned out very differently.'

'You are telling me,' Cynthia frowned, 'that perhaps Malcolm Everson and Faun Moran were brought to that spot, that their car was then pushed over the cliff, that Malcolm's body was dumped as though it had fallen from the car and whoever this young woman was, her body was then set on fire in the hope that . . . Well, presumably in the hope that it would cover up another crime. The murder of this girl, I suppose. But how would Faun fit into such a conspiracy? You can't for one moment think she was complicit?'

'That's something else we can't be sure of, not yet,' Henry told her. 'What we know so far is that the car went over the cliff edge, that Malcolm Everson was certainly badly hurt, either while he was still in the car or perhaps when he tumbled over the cliff edge. That there was a young woman, whose identity we do not yet have, found at the scene and an attempt had been made to burn her body and to burn the car. Those are the facts, as we currently know them. Interpretation of those findings is still not quite possible. However, when we have the post-mortem report on Faun Moran and the post-mortem is carried out on this other young woman, I believe things will become a little clearer.'

'She's been six months in her grave,' Cynthia objected. 'Well in *a* grave, as it turns out, poor child, it's not her own, is it. What condition will the body be in?'

'Not good, I would guess. She has been inside a coffin, inside a mausoleum. It is very possible that the body will be still in a state where a post-mortem will tell us how she died, and if she was still alive when the fire began. Anyway, something might be discovered that is of use to us. I would dearly like to know who she is and it's possible that dental records might still be of some use, even though the face and head were severely damaged. We weren't meant to know; whoever dumped her body went to a great deal of trouble to conceal the identity. And if our farmer, Mr Carter, is correct, then someone deliberately set out to smash her features so badly that identification was impossible.'

'That's a terrible thought, Henry. It's callous. I can't believe that Caius Moran did not want a post-mortem carried out at the time. Surely that would have saved everybody a lot of trouble?'

'In retrospect it would have done, but at the time it was assumed to have been a tragic accident and neither family wanted more scandal attached than was inevitable. If we're being charitable, which I'm inclined not to be where Moran is concerned, the family simply wanted to grieve in private and Malcolm Everson's family was simply so shocked they too wanted to retreat from the reality of it all. So they removed him to the sanatorium where he was out of sight and out of mind, I suppose. It seems only his sister Violet bothers to visit.'

'I like Violet. She has a good head on her shoulders. This is a terrible business, Henry, perhaps not a good way of returning to work.'

Mickey was amused. 'No, we should probably have arranged a nice simple little murder for him,' he said. 'Someone known to the victim, bashing the victim over the head, how would that have been?'

Cynthia laughed. 'I don't suppose you get many of those.'

'The local constabularies are usually perfectly capable of dealing with the simple crimes. It's more complex ones like this that require the services of Sergeant Mickey Hitchens and Chief Inspector Johnstone,' Mickey told her pompously. Then he grinned at Cynthia. 'We'll sort it, you see if we don't.'

Henry had played a hunch – that Caxton's factotum, Victor Mullins, might have a record. In that he'd been disappointed, but his second hunch that there might be some record of him as a boxer, had he actually had professional fights, had paid off. He'd asked that someone be sent to do a round of the newspaper morgues and consult the sports sections and that turned up the goods. Vic Mullins indeed had a professional record and, better still, had on occasion been photographed after a successful bout.

Morning brought a messenger, and that messenger brought a photograph, and after breakfast Mickey was dispatched early, in the hope of catching the menfolk before they left for work, to speak with Mr and Mrs Colin Chambers and their neighbours, the Fullers, to ask if this looked like the man on the beach.

'And they said it might well be,' Mickey told Henry as he devoured his delayed breakfast. 'Mrs Fuller was certain and her friend, Mrs Chambers, also convinced. The husbands are not willing to commit, but do admit to the possibility.'

'Which is less than I'd hoped, but what I'd expected. And we have to ask ourselves how many other men of that height and build are even remotely connected to this affair? So far, none.'

'And we don't know that this one is. I'd be more inclined to be impressed if they'd seen his face more clearly. But from the distance they were at it's only going to be an impression of height and build that strikes a chord. And even then we can't be certain their reports are accurate. Witnesses usually report those suspected of violence as being bigger and more powerful than is usual. I'd be happier if someone else had noticed an exceptionally large man wandering around on Bournemouth seafront on that Sunday morning. You'd expect him to stick out like a sore thumb and instead of that this is the only sighting. While I believe the witnesses to be perfectly genuine and to be doing their best to be of help, they are also aware that we want them to have seen this potential suspect; a man already looming perhaps too large in their imaginations for their reports to be one hundred per cent accurate.'

'Which we both know no witness ever is,' Henry agreed. He looked again at the picture of Vic Mullins. He'd won his bout and stood with one arm raised, looming over his unfortunate opponent, who now lay spark out on the canvas. The referee, himself not insignificant, allowed some sense of scale but, Henry asked himself, had he seen this man in isolation, standing on the sand with the body of a slight young woman in his arms, would he have been truly able to guess at his height or be accurate as to his build?

'It was worth asking the question,' he said, aware that he sounded a little despondent.

'It's always worth asking the question. Now, we have a train to catch,' Mickey reminded him. 'I don't suppose it's worth asking Cynthia if she can put her dislike of the man aside and arrange an appointment with this Ben Caxton fellow?'

'No,' Henry said, thinking about the conversation he'd had with Cynthia about Ben Caxton. 'I think we might organize this one ourselves.'

TWELVE

The full post-mortem report on Faun Moran was waiting for them when they returned to London. It confirmed that the cause of death had been a broken neck but chose not to speculate on whether this had been accidental or deliberate. There was also bruising to the skull, not enough to cause death or even unconsciousness, but which might indicate a fall and which was therefore suggestive of a struggle or an attack.

'So she hit her head and perhaps broke her neck at the same time?' Henry pondered. 'Or she fell and hit her head and someone then broke her neck. Either is possible. The way her body was deposited on the beach indicates perhaps remorse, certainly concern. The body could easily have been concealed, buried, simply discarded and the chances are we would never have known. No, someone wants the truth to come out.'

'If that's the case, why don't they come forward?' Mickey asked.

'That's the question, isn't it? Did that man on the beach kill her? Did he know who did, or does he know for certain that it was an accidental death? And what is he afraid of that is making him reluctant to speak out?'

'Could have been any number of reasons. But I think we can assume he was concerned about the girl, that his association with her was more than just someone sent out to get rid of the body.'

There had also been evidence of recent sexual activity. Rough sex, the surgeon speculated. There was bruising to thighs and vulva.

'Rape?' Mickey asked. 'He seems reluctant to say that, but the inference is there.'

'And there are other signs of violence. Broken and newly

healed ribs and a still-broken wrist. Mickey, this girl has been missing since the end of June – do we believe that over that entire time she had been abused and tortured?' The idea horrified him. It was beyond anything he had contemplated.

'And why have there been no reports, no sightings, not even false sightings that have stood up to any scrutiny? No one has seen a tall, solidly built man anywhere else, in Bournemouth or along the coast. The description has gone out in the local papers, there have even been artists' impressions produced and he *is* distinctive. Even allowing for unconscious exaggeration on the part of the witnesses, we know he is strong enough to have carried that poor young woman from the car, along the beach and to have stood with her as though she weighed nothing until choosing to put her down. And that only when he felt he'd attracted enough attention to himself.'

'We have to hope that the injuries were not evidence of long-term mistreatment,' Mickey said sternly, though Henry could hear that he didn't believe a word of his own protests. 'As to lack of witnesses, perhaps his very distinctiveness is the problem. An average man, of average height, and average build, with average eyes and hair will produce many sightings because there are so many people who fit the picture. You start asking about a man who is well over six feet, very broad in the shoulder, built like a brick outhouse, in fact, and there won't be so many mistakes on behalf of the public. You either see a man that size and shape or you don't.'

Henry supposed that he had a point. But the more he thought about what Faun Moran may have suffered, the more he felt his own distress. He thought about Melissa and what might have become of her had Henry not been able to track her kidnapper down and bring her safely home. And no one had even known that Faun Moran was missing, had, as now seemed likely, been detained against her will and treated with such violence.

He took a deep breath and told himself that he must focus on the present moment and not on what he could not now prevent.

Arrangements had been made that the body of the unknown girl would be removed from the Moran grave that afternoon;

perhaps the subsequent post-mortem would at least provide some leads.

Mid-afternoon found them visiting the lodgings that Faun Moran had previously shared with the Cooper sisters, Fliss and Bo, or Felicity and Belinda as their parents knew them. A third girl now slept in the room that had been Faun's, but she was absent.

'She works,' Fliss told Henry, her eyes widening slightly as though this was an unusual idea. 'In a gallery, so it's not like an ordinary job.'

'And you and your sister don't?' Henry asked.

'Lord, no, Daddy is loaded, so there's no need. I expect we'll both marry in a year or two, but for now we're free and easy.'

Henry bristled slightly but tried to keep his emotions under control.

'I say,' Bo said, 'it's a bit of a rum do, isn't it? I mean we all thought that Faun, well you know, that Faun was dead. And now she is. Again. Will they have another funeral, do you think?'

'I imagine they will,' Mickey told her. 'I imagine everyone is very shocked,' he suggested and Bo and Fliss exchanged a glance and then decided to look suitably so.

Henry sighed and accepted the invitation to sit down and make himself comfortable. He decided to leave the questions to his sergeant who undoubtedly had more patience with frivolous young women than Henry was ever able to summon.

'Miss Pat Moran, Faun's sister, suggested that Faun might have been seeing someone new. Perhaps an older man. She suggested that it might have been serious.'

Fliss shrugged. 'She might have been, I suppose,' she said cautiously. 'Faun usually had someone on the go.'

'I want you to understand,' Mickey told them, 'that your friend is now dead, that her neck was broken, that she was left on a beach to be found by strangers. And this was some months after you all believed her to have been deceased. I want you to imagine where she might have been in that time, and why she had not been in contact with any of you, not her friends or her family. Suppose for one moment that she was being prevented, that your friend was in trouble for all this time, perhaps hurt and suffering and you didn't know and could offer her no help. Surely you would want us to find out what happened to her and point us in the direction of anyone else that might know something?'

Fliss blinked. 'Oh, Lordy,' she said. 'When you put it like that, I suppose it is a terrible thing. I mean, we had no idea that she wasn't dead, you know? I mean, we all thought that she'd just gone out for a drive with her friend and had gone off the road. Though we did think it was very strange. I mean, Mal never drank very much, and he was such a careful driver. He was boring, we all said that – that's why we were all so surprised. And then he's been locked away all this time, like he's gone crazy or something, like his family don't want to know. Well, it makes you think, doesn't it?'

Henry thought that they were drifting somewhat from the original subject and Mickey clearly agreed. 'And do you think she was seeing someone? Someone older, someone her family might not approve of?'

'Well, I suppose . . . I suppose they might not have liked it. The thing is Faun liked to do things that were, I mean not against the law or anything, but which were a bit of fun. Which were a bit . . . adventurous, if you know what I mean.'

'We believe she frequented the Gargoyle and other nightclubs. She was very young to be allowed on those premises.'

'Well, it depends who you're with, of course. If you're with someone older, if you're with the right kind of people, no one turns a hair.'

'And would Faun have been with these right kind of people?'

'Of course, silly. How else would she have got in?'

'And do these people have names?' Mickey's tone was light, amused.

The girls laughed. 'Everybody has a name,' Bo said.

'Perhaps you could make a list for me of Faun's particular friends. No one will be in any trouble, I promise you that. All we're doing is looking for information, trying to understand how Faun lived in the weeks and months before she disappeared.'

Fliss and Bo exchanged a glance once again and it seemed to Henry that something more serious passed between them this time.

'Look,' Bo said, 'after she died, I mean after she died in the car crash, I mean after we *thought* she died in the car crash, they sent for her things. Her family, I mean, and of course we packed everything up in her cases, and we made it ready for collecting but while we were going through her things . . .' She looked anxiously at her sister and then at Mickey. Henry was ignored. He held his peace.

'While you were going through her things,' Mickey prompted.

'Well, we found some letters. Love letters. We read them and we decided that perhaps they weren't very suitable for giving back to her family. They were, well . . . not exactly smutty, but I don't think her father would have enjoyed reading them. I don't think her family were ever intended to see them, so we didn't send them.'

'Did we do right?' Fliss asked.

'I think you probably did,' Mickey assured her. 'And what happened to these letters?'

'We did intend to get rid of them, to burn them or something, but we never quite got around to it. You know how these things are – you think about doing something and then it slips your mind.'

Henry twitched but sat still. Mickey leaned forward confidentially. 'And you still have these letters?'

'Yes, but should we really be giving them to police officers? They *are* personal, they *are* love letters.'

'And if they might help us find out what happened to your friend, why she disappeared, where she was, if she was kept there against her will? How she died?'

'I doubt they'll tell you that, but I suppose we can give them to you. But don't give them to her father. He wouldn't understand at all.'

'I won't do that,' Mickey assured her.

Fliss went through to another room. As the door opened a cloud of perfume and powder drifted through so Henry guessed this must be one of their bedrooms. She returned with the bundle of letters tied with blue ribbon and handed them to Mickey, together with a very flirtatious smile.

I might as well not be here, Henry thought, and was somewhat amused at the impression his sergeant seemed to have made.

In the car heading back to Scotland Yard they began to examine the heavy cream envelopes. This was not cheap stationery, nor was it the sort of thing that Henry would have thought a young person would choose. Laid paper, watermarked though not monogrammed. The letters written in a fluent and elegant hand.

'No address,' Mickey commented, 'but I suppose if the girl knew where they were coming from it would not be necessary. Just a date, and a single initial: R?'

'Hopefully there will be some clue in the letters. There's what, a dozen of them?'

'And we have a list of friends and close associates that her family didn't seem to know about,' Mickey agreed. 'She was so visible, so much part of the social scene and yet she is as hard to pin down as sea mist. It seems to me, Henry, that everybody saw her but nobody actually looked at her, if you know what I mean. What close friends did she have? I would have expected her sister or the Coopers to know that but all they seem to have known is a list of acquaintances and fellow partygoers. And it's clear that Fliss and Bo Cooper did not mix in the same circles. Faun Moran may have shared the rent but she does not seem to have shared their lives. Everyone tells us that Faun was adventurous, or unconventional, or daring, but no one so far has managed to explain what they mean by that, unless it's that she went to gambling clubs and chose to dance in places with less than salubrious reputations.'

'And how did this other young woman fit into the story? Why has she not been reported missing?'

'Most likely she has, but we simply don't know where she came from so we have no idea where to look for those reports. What I don't understand, Henry, is how a man cannot recognize his own daughter. True, if the face was damaged there may have been difficulties, but would you not recognize the hands, the general demeanour, that overall look that each person possesses and that makes them unique?'

'We don't even know if the father viewed the body,' Henry realized, 'or who made the formal identification. It's possible that whoever did simply accepted the facts as they seemed to present themselves. Even Pat said that the body was unrecognizable, and she was genuinely fond of her sister. If she did not recognize her—'

'Pat was overcome by horror,' Mickey objected. 'How did she explain it . . . that her sister was broken, damaged beyond all recognition. Perhaps their father too was overcome by horror. Perhaps we can be charitable.'

'I see no reason to be charitable. The man is an arrogant idiot.'

'Arrogant maybe. He can't be that much of an idiot, not if you look at his business empire. There must be brains in that head somewhere.'

Henry scowled at his sergeant but then admitted, 'Brains of some sort, I suppose. So, how do we proceed from here? What do we have today that we did not have yesterday?'

'A list of associates and the venues where they like to be seen, even if the Cooper sisters were unaware of addresses, or workplaces, or even second names in many cases. So we can begin by looking for the names on this list, in the places they like to frequent. Assuming these places are still as fashionable as they were last year, of course. And we look for this mysterious R, we read the letters and we see what can be gleaned. And we hope that someone sees our big man with the broad shoulders who left Faun Moran's body on the beach. We do what we always do, Henry, we follow what leads we have and we hope that luck is also on our side.'

THIRTEEN

Faun, December

M y only change is when he lets me go downstairs to have a bath. I have to take my chances then, scream and kick and make as much noise as I can and just hope that someone hears me and that when they hear me they come running.

But will they?

Even little Martha believes that I am just too crazy for words. She believes that I have had some kind of brain fever and that anything I say is therefore half lies, or at least untruths because I can no longer tell the difference. Her pity of me is so painful. She sat with me one night when things had gone too far with HIM. He had hurt me so badly and my ribs hurt so much that I could scarcely breathe. Martha believed that I had done it to myself. That I had somehow got out of my room and thrown myself down the stairs. How could she believe that her kind and caring master had been the one to do that? I could not tell her about the other things that he has done.

That he and Vic have done.

Now she tells me that she will be leaving soon and though I shall miss her dreadfully I see a means of getting help. I have almost convinced her to send a letter for me. To send a letter to Pat, to you, my sweetest sister. I know that you will come and find me if you only know that I am still alive.

If I can convince her to do this one small thing for me. This one big, massive, special thing. This dangerous thing that I'm afraid to ask in case she tells him. Then I might just make it out of here alive.

Friday 17 January

The next few days were busy but not particularly productive so far as Henry was concerned. They began by contacting those on the lists given by Pat, Mrs Belmont, and then by the Cooper sisters. Intelligence from these sources added contact details to others on the list. This all, Henry considered, simply added to the mass of information they had that led absolutely nowhere.

Henry divided his data into three sets. He found that it fell naturally into these categories and that the names of their different lists grouped into firstly 'Friends of the Belmonts', who were the well-off, influential, but not quite out of the top drawer. The second group were the 'Hangers On', as he found himself calling them, who were not a natural fit into the Belmont society and comprised artists and writers and even a few professionals such as bank managers and physicians who found themselves nominally accepted, because of something particular they had to offer.

Elements of this group also crossed over into his third category, as he found that writers and artists and those from the acting profession often did. The third category was perhaps the hardest for him to reach and to interview, comprising as they did members of the 'Bright Young Things' but also their elders. Older brothers and sisters, parents, suppliers of those allowances which allowed younger siblings to run riot across the city.

'They don't exactly run riot,' Mickey observed.

'They don't? There have been reports of up to fifty cars and their occupants participating in one of their so-called scavenger hunts. Young women chasing through the London Underground in search of some fresh sport or other, some clue their friends have left. That is as close to running riot as makes no matter.' He saw the amusement on his sergeant's face and sat back in his chair with a sigh. 'I want to be out there and doing, Mickey, not shuffling paper and speaking on the telephone to people who can offer me nothing more than fake condolences and assurances that they would help me if they could. And have you seen the newspapers?'

'I have indeed; we feature most prominently.'

'And that doesn't bother you?'

'Why should it? We do our job, which is investigating the crime. The newspapers do their job, which is to report the most scandalous elements and if they can't find any scandalous elements they make them up.'

'I wish I could be as sanguine,' Henry complained.

'You may take comfort from the fact that the newspapers are mostly rehashing those elements about the early investigation that they now know to be incorrect. When Faun Moran was falsely declared to be deceased. It is the first investigation, such as it was, that comes out badly and about which the press are most scathing. Most now express the belief that with Detective Chief Inspector Johnstone and his faithful Sergeant Hitchens on the case a solution will be found and all will again be right with the world.'

Grinning at his boss, Mickey pulled out a chair and sat himself down. 'What point is there in getting annoyed? But while you are in this mood I'll give you something else to be cross about so we can get it all over and done with.'

'And what is that?'

'We made the assumption, did we not, that Caius Moran must've identified the body of his own daughter and it seems he did not.'

Henry sat bolt upright. 'What? Why would he hand such a task over to someone else? So who did identify her?'

'Oh, it gets better. It seems the family doctor was dispatched and according to a statement we have, from said family doctor when I spoke to him about an hour ago, he told Mr Moran that he believed *in all probability* the body in the car was Faun Moran but that the head was too badly damaged to be of use in identification. He asserted, or so he says, that anything he could report would be purely circumstantial, predicated on the fact that Miss Moran got into the car and was wearing the same jewellery. That the young woman in the car was approximately the same height and build, so far as he could tell, but that he had not actually seen Miss Moran for at least three years as she was, and I quote, "an uncommonly healthy young lady".'

Henry was staring at him. 'And did Moran give some excuse for not attending to this task himself?'

'It would seem that both he and the elder brother were away on business. I don't know where, because the doctor did not know where, but a telegram had been sent informing them of the girl's death and a telegram was sent back requesting the doctor do the necessary. The doctor made the identification, the body was shipped off to the undertaker and was interred at a private ceremony. This happened only three days after the car crash.'

'A private ceremony? But Cynthia and others we have spoken to went to the funeral.'

'No, if you remember she said they went to the memorial service. That she *saw* only where the body had been interred. The body itself had already been placed in the mausoleum, but the memorial service seems to have been organized as though the poor unfortunate young woman's body was still present, along the lines of a normal funeral service. The doctor, who was present, tells me it was a very grand affair.'

'But only three days after the crash? The inquest had not yet been held. And we know that no post-mortem was carried out. This was all very irregular.'

'I raised this with the doctor and he pointed out, as it seems Mr Moran had already done to him, that the body was merely placed in the coffin and interred in the family mausoleum. She had not been embalmed. The body was examined by the police surgeon and death was pronounced. Her own doctor viewed the body and asserted that death must have been as a result of the crash. Should the body be required for further investigation, it could, theoretically have been made available. It seems Mr Moran has religious objections to post-mortems. It seems he also has the money to pay off any officials or to make appropriate donations so that nobody seemed to raise objections.'

'Pay off what officials, what donation? Why would he even do that?'

'As to why, you'd have to ask him, and good luck with that. As far as the payments are concerned, this is something the doctor said in passing and a statement he then tried to rescind. I think the doctor was annoyed to have been put in such a position, especially as it's likely the press would make a meal of it should they know. It is enough for the press to make a meal of, Henry. A man who does not even wish to identify the body of his own child, whether estranged or not, and a doctor who does not know his own patient but just assumes that the dead girl was who he was told she ought to be.'

Henry narrowed his eyes and peered closely at his sergeant. 'Do you believe this is likely to become known to the press?'

Mickey tipped his chair back on two legs, balancing experimentally before clunking it back down again. 'Who knows what the newspapers will print,' he said. 'What anonymous sources might let slip.'

Henry glared for a moment and then laughed. 'I'm not sure if that would help or hinder our investigation.'

'It will stir things up,' Mickey told him. 'And it will deflect a little of the heat from the original investigation. I'm not seeing this as a favour to DI Shelton. But the local officers certainly deserve more credit than they have been given and I think there should be a report on that as well. Scotland Yard did not give the finest account of itself on that occasion but the local constabulary did an excellent job, so far as they were allowed.'

'You are sailing close to the wind, Mickey.'

'Why? What have I done? This place leaks like a sieve, you know that.'

'This place only leaks when someone pierces it from the inside.'

A constable arrived and handed Henry a folder. It contained the post-mortem report of the young woman who had been found in the car, the young woman who had been burnt and her body had been mistaken for that of Faun Moran. Henry laid it on the table so they could both look at it.

'So she did not die of smoke inhalation or of burning, that is a mercy at least,' Mickey said. 'Cause of death isn't clear. There are injuries to her legs and body consistent with being hit by a car – though the surgeon states that can only be speculation. He believes most, if not all, of the injuries to the head and neck to have occurred after death but again stresses that this is speculation. And he suggests that had photographs of the crime scene been available then our task and his might be easier. So where are those damned photographs? I think perhaps I'll go and speak to the lads in the evidence store, just on the off chance.'

'We are lucky to have anything after all this time,' Henry said. 'In terms of identifying marks, she had previously broken a leg, but that's a commonplace enough injury and we do not have any idea where she was treated. Do we know what happened to the clothing? To whatever the girl was wearing before she was interred?'

Mickey shook his head. 'I'll speak to the undertaker. But my guess is they will have been destroyed, or otherwise disposed of. What was left of them after the fire had taken its share. From the state of the corpse I doubt there would have been anything much left. The fire had consumed hair and skin over perhaps ninety per cent of the body. The post-mortem suggests that she was drenched in accelerant which would explain the smell of petrol. But whoever did this, did not do such a thorough job as they intended. Time was not on their side and so their work was sloppy and overly swift.'

'And Carter and his son-in-law were overly efficient and overly brave,' Henry said. 'I guarantee most people would simply have seen the fire and run as fast as they could in the opposite direction.'

He glanced through the rest of the report. 'There's not a great deal more of use to us,' he said. 'The girl was of similar height to Faun, perhaps just a little heavier, but one thing is for certain – the dress that Faun was wearing when she was left on the beach did not belong to this girl. That was made for someone taller and plumper.'

'And richer than this girl, if we're judging by the compact.'

'That's true. It had just occurred to me that it would amuse whoever is responsible for all this to dress one girl in the clothing of the other. The girl in the car must have been similarly dressed to Faun Moran if they were to have had any hope of the deception being accepted.'

'Though had the body been fully burnt, it wouldn't really matter what the girl was wearing and no doubt that was the intent.'

'True,' Henry conceded.

'You're not voicing your more disturbing thought,' Mickey

stated. 'That the beaded dress and patent shoes belonged to a third girl, that there may well be a third girl missing. And if there is, then her identity is as much a mystery as that of the girl in the car. And if a third girl is missing, what is there to prevent there being a fourth or even a fifth?'

'If you don't mind we will put that aside for the moment,' Henry told him. 'I have no doubt we will need to deal with this possibility, but for the moment two dead girls is enough.'

Henry turned back to the stack of love letters that had sat on his desk since they had returned from their visit to the Cooper sisters. 'We are still no closer to knowing who this mysterious R might be,' he said. 'On the lists we have there are Richards, Robins, Roberts and even a Ralph, all of whom deny sending the letters or having anything more than a casual, passing association with Faun Moran. And of course one of them might be lying, but without bringing them in for interview there is no way of discovering that and even then all they have to do is hold their nerve and we'll get no further. And this set has plenty of nerve to hold. All but one are married men, and all are respectable.'

'With a capital R. And so we are also warned not to be heavy-handed with these respectable men. Have any agreed to submit handwriting samples?'

'Yes, several in fact, which is at least helpful. I have asked for permission to release a sample of the handwriting from the letters to the press, but the deputy commissioner is reluctant to do so for fear of embarrassing a perfectly innocent party. He points out that as the recipient of the letters is never actually mentioned by name, they might not even be Faun Moran's. It's possible that someone entrusted them to her keeping because they didn't want a husband or father to see them.'

'An unlikely scenario, I'd have thought.'

'Agreed, but we have been told to tread carefully, there are wealthy and influential people involved in all of this and the deputy commissioner considers there is enough scandal attached already, with the failure of the original investigation. I don't know, Mickey. I feel as though we are being blocked at every turn. What do you make of the letters?'

Mickey took the topmost, slid it out of its envelope and unfolded it, laid it on the table and began to read.

> My dearest sweet darling,
> I cannot tell you how much the hours will drag until I see you again. You brighten my day with your smile and your laughter makes my heart feel as though it will explode.

'And so they go on, page after page, letter after letter,' he said dryly. 'If you ask me they are so overblown as to be unbelievable and absolutely designed to turn the head of a teenaged girl who, by all accounts, has been left with little guidance, has only minimal contact with her family, and seems to have very few true friends. I don't doubt that her sister Pat loved her very dearly, but Pat has a family of her own and couldn't be expected to nursemaid a younger sister who had absolutely no intention of being protected or of listening to the voice of experience.'

'I suspect youth usually believes it knows best,' Henry agreed. 'And I have to admit on occasion it does. Sometimes we can get set in our ways and forget that once upon a time we had the courage of our own youthful convictions and that conviction often carried us through.'

'My, we are feeling jaundiced today.'

'Jaundiced indeed. I'm feeling the strain of knowing that two and perhaps three young women are dead, and that every direction I look, every lead we follow, seems either to go nowhere or to end in a wall of marshmallow, that just absorbs our efforts.'

'But if it's marshmallow we have we'll just have to eat our way through it,' Mickey told him.

Vic

She had arrived one night out of the blue, driving that little car of hers at speed down the lane and skidding to a halt at the foot of the steps. It had been raining, Vic remembered, raining heavily and in only her thin silk dress she was soaked through by the time she had reached the door.

The commotion her arrival had created had drawn Vic into the front hall and she had flung herself at him. 'I'm never going home. I'm never going back there again.'

'What happened? Tell me what happened.'

'I want to see Ben; I want to talk to him. I want to talk to him now.'

She had never, Vic had thought, sounded more like a petulant child. Any illusion of Faun as a grown woman fell away. She was angry and tearful and sounded, he thought, more like an infant of five or six.

He was about to tell her that Ben could not be disturbed when his employer appeared at the head of the stairs and motioned that they should both come up.

'Sit down,' he had told her when they had all assembled in Ben's private sitting room. 'Here, drink this. Tell me, what's been going on?'

She had taken the brandy glass and cradled it between her hands. She was shivering now and Vic had thrown a rug around her shoulders but she seemed oblivious of him. She had eyes only for Ben. 'He's threatening to cancel my allowance, and not to pay the rent on my flat unless I behave, as he puts it. He said I was behaving like . . . like a whore. Me, his own daughter, and he says something like that. He says I flirt too much. That I've been seen in unsuitable places.'

'Well, in his eyes, both of those things are probably true.' Ben sounded flippant, unconcerned, and she was furious.

'You were the one that took me there, to those places!'

'And that was probably wrong of me. You are just a child, after all. Perhaps I should apologize to your father. Though I think if he knew that I was responsible for your insubordination, I would have heard about it by now. I doubt he realizes that I was involved so perhaps we should keep it that way. He would definitely not approve of that.'

She had stared at him, uncomprehending. She had come to Ben believing that he would stand up for her and all he was doing was making fun. 'That's a lousy thing to say, it's all hokum. I thought you were my friend.'

Ben came close, knelt down beside her chair. 'Of course

I'm your friend. We are all friends here. And we all know you've done nothing to be ashamed of.'

Somewhat mollified, she had allowed him to take her hand and when he had suggested that they all have a late supper she had agreed. And then when he had suggested that she remained there for the night instead of driving back to London she had agreed to that too, on condition that she was in her own room, of course. And Ben had laughed. 'There will be no impropriety, I promise you that.'

And Vic had seen how disappointed she had looked. Ben could have asked her to do anything at that moment and she would have acquiesced.

FOURTEEN

Saturday 18 January

On the Saturday evening Henry went with Cynthia and Albert to the Savoy. They had travelled up to London and booked in for the night and taken Henry as a guest to a party they had been invited to. Halfway through the evening and Henry was still not entirely sure what they were celebrating but the food was good, as was the wine, and there were several people present from the lists with whom Henry had failed to gain an interview or even a telephone conversation.

Cynthia had suggested that he beard them in their own environment, where introductions could properly be made and they would be more open to his advances.

This was not even Cynthia's usual environment; it was a little upmarket even for her and many of the guests were from old and titled families and would not normally have given house room to his sister and her husband, they being new money and from trade. But Cynthia had been invited to this party by Marguerite Perdue, whose wildly romantic novels were very much in vogue and whose circle included lords and ladies, writers and artists and those with whom she shared charitable concerns. This put Cynthia almost on a level with this old money – at least for a few hours.

The author was also, Henry gathered, a good friend of Cynthia's and they had known each other since Marguerite had simply been Maggie Purdy and they had studied shorthand and typing at the same evening class. He guessed she was one of the few present who could claim such long acquaintance.

When the formal part of the evening was over and the dancing had begun Cynthia took the time to make introductions and Henry discovered that 'my brother, the murder detective' opened doors and conversation that had hitherto been closed to him. Of course, everybody now wanted to talk about Faun Moran and the great mystery of her death, her mysterious reappearance and murder. She was, after all, one of their own and young, beautiful and now at the heart of a mystery that almost seemed as romantic as one of their hostess' novels. Or was that his cynicism speaking? Henry wondered. It also didn't hurt, Henry realized, that his most recent investigation, in which he had been injured when rescuing his niece, was also fresh in the minds of many who knew Cynthia and were desperate to get the inside story of what had gone on and who lost no time telling how brave he must have been. Henry was not used to being cast as hero and it grated now, but he was wise enough to realize this gave him an opening.

It was easy to turn the conversation to young Faun Moran. 'Such a sweet girl, a little foolish, of course, but who isn't at that age. She was such a beautiful debutante, of course. A lot of young women don't bother with that kind of thing anymore, and we all know it can be tedious, but she knew her mother would have wanted her to be presented. I remember her mother the year she came out. What a beauty she was.'

'Of course there are all sorts of rumours about his business. They say he lost an absolute pile when the stock market crashed.'

'You shouldn't listen to rumours, my dear, but I have heard he's been rationalizing. Isn't that the word they use?'

'What, for selling off the family silver?'

'Did dear Faun have any special friends?' The tilt of the head. A moment of careful consideration.

'Well, there was young Tommy Hillby, of course.'

'Oh no, she finished with him an age ago. He's engaged now, I believe.'

'And there were rumours of those dreadful parties, of course.' The speaker leaned in confidentially towards Cynthia and whispered, 'Petting parties, you know, come over from America. Of course, the worst things always do.'

Cynthia did her best to look shocked but then whispered back, 'From what I've heard, what happens at these parties is far more innocent than it sounds. Though I'm told that a pettable girl is called a biscuit. Can you imagine that? I could see that leading to all sorts of misunderstandings.'

Henry tried not to roll his eyes. He allowed the hilarity to die down before he asked, 'So you don't think she was serious about anybody?'

The dowager he was speaking to and whose name he had not quite caught pulled thoughtfully on her earring and then said, 'The person to ask, of course, is young Ben Caxton. Nice boy, such a pity about his face and hands. And his eye, of course. I did hear that he'd set his cap at Pat Moran, but of course she threw him over and married young Clifford. It was not a bad match; he's a decent enough young fellow and they do seem happy from what I can tell. But I suppose because he liked the elder sister, he took an interest in the younger. Ben Caxton, I mean, not Clifford. He's here tonight, of course, I saw him not a half hour ago.'

She slipped her hand through Henry's arm. 'Come with me, my dear, and I will make the introductions.'

Henry caught the amused look on his sister's face across the room as he was led away. She raised a hand and gave him a little wave and then went off to find her husband. Henry knew that Cynthia had been willing to make this introduction herself, but he knew also that she would be glad to be relieved of the responsibility. He realized also that any introduction made by this dowager would be more acceptable to Ben Caxton himself and would perhaps appeal to his vanity.

Ben Caxton was holding court, surrounded by a group of opulently dressed men and women who were laughing at something he had said. He noticed Henry, tilted his head to one side and looked thoughtfully at this man he did not know and around whose arm Millicent Pavis's clawlike hand was wrapped. He excused himself from the group and Henry could almost hear the sigh of disappointment as they released him.

'Millicent, how are you, my dear? And what have you brought me? I don't think I've had the pleasure.'

'I've brought you a detective.' Millicent sounded very proud of the fact. 'We've all been discussing poor Faun Moran and I told him if anybody knows anything it would be you. You know everything about everybody.'

'Hardly that. Millicent, you were always prone to exaggeration.' Ben Caxton extended a hand and introduced himself.

'Henry Johnstone,' Henry said.

'Detective Chief Inspector Henry Johnstone,' Millicent emphasized. She released Henry's arm and patted him gently. 'Now you two have a good chat, it's been so lovely to make your acquaintance.'

The two men watched her go, disappearing into the crowd. Ben Caxton laughed. 'You mustn't mind Millicent, she's quite a character. Now, can I get you a drink? Let's try and find somewhere quiet to sit, if that's possible in this crush.'

He glanced around and then began to walk across the ballroom towards what Henry could now see was an anteroom at the side. The crowd seemed to part before him and Henry got the strangest feeling that if he didn't hurry to keep up the sea of bodies would simply close between him and Ben Caxton and he would be cut off and he would be becalmed.

Caxton directed Henry to a seat, beckoning a waiter as he did so and asking Henry what he would like to drink. 'And now, what can I do for you?'

'I'd like to ask you about Faun Moran. How well did you know her? How close were the two of you?'

Ben Caxton raised an eyebrow. Somehow, he was still handsome and certainly charismatic, Henry thought, despite the scars and his missing eye. He wore an eye patch which gave him a slightly piratical air and on the scarred side of his face the skin was pulled tight. The scars extended down on to his neck and Henry guessed continued on to his shoulder and chest. His right hand, Henry noticed as he took his glass, was also badly mutilated with two fingers missing and thick ridges of badly healed tissue crisscrossing the back.

Other men, Henry thought, would hide in the shadows and be reluctant to expose their injuries, but Ben Caxton gave the impression that he was a man almost oblivious to them. That he had undoubtedly earned these questionable badges of honour with acts of valour, but was not going to make a big fuss about it. Henry reminded himself that Caxton had gained his scars by saving the lives of others and had almost died in the effort.

He took his own whiskey and soda and then said, 'I understand you knew the older sister, Pat Moran as she was. Pat Clifford now.'

'I know the family. The father and I have often done business. Though not so much the past year or so when our interests diverged. Pat is a wonderful woman, happily married with two beautiful children. And I have to say she deserves the happiness. Caius gave her a hard time growing up.' He paused, as though hesitant about what he was going to say next and then added, 'Nothing is ever good enough for Caius. He is a hard man in many ways.'

'And the younger daughter, Faun, she pulled against that constraint.'

'From what I observed, she certainly did.'

'And what is your opinion of the girl? I believe you took an interest.'

'An interest!' A short bark of laughter. 'I liked her elder sister and for a time, as no doubt you have heard, I wondered if she would begin to like me as much. As it happened she found someone more to her taste, but we remain good friends and I have a lot of respect for Pat. So when Faun came on the scene, yes, I took an interest. She seemed like a very unhappy child, and make no mistake, Chief Inspector, she was a child. Naive, oddly unworldly. In some ways, of course, that was charming but it's also very dangerous, there are always people around to take advantage and I worried for her, I will admit that. So yes, I suppose I became like a big brother.'

'And no more than that.'

'As I said, she was just a child.'

'She was nineteen. Girls are frequently married at that age.'

'The more fool them. And the men they marry. Girls are rushed into these things, they have no chance to discover who they are before suddenly they are wives and mothers and more than often unhappy. I must admit I worried for Pat. She was only twenty-one, you know, when she married Clifford, but it has worked out well for her.'

'From what I've heard Faun was fond of . . . unconventional venues. She was often to be found in what might be called inappropriate places, gambling clubs and less than salubrious dance halls.'

Ben Caxton laughed. 'Oh my goodness, you do sound like a prude. I would not have expected that of Cynthia's brother. Oh yes, I know who you are. Now there is a woman to be admired,' he added, his eyes on Henry, and Henry knew that Caxton was gauging his response.

Keeping his voice neutral, Henry said, 'She is remarkable.'

'Quite so. I've no doubt that Faun would have been equally remarkable had she lived, but of course we will never know now. You must be aggrieved, I imagine, at how badly the incident was handled. The car crash, I mean. It does not reflect well on the police force, and now you are taking over the enquiry I imagine it does not reflect well on you. It seems to me that this is a little bit of a poisoned chalice.'

'You could see it, as I am inclined to, as an opportunity to put things right. Mistakes were made. There were misjudgements and not just by the police. It would for instance have been helpful if a full post-mortem had been carried out rather than a simple, cursory examination. The identification could have been called into question much sooner. But apparently Mr Moran did not even take the time to identify his own daughter. He gave that task to the family doctor, who proved unequal to it.'

Henry knew that he was being provocative. He watched as the unscarred side of Ben Caxton's mouth twitched into a smile. 'Oh, you are as fierce as your sister,' he said. 'But that is no bad thing. I believe Caius was away from home and thought that the matter could be better expedited by having the doctor make the identification immediately, rather than wait for his return. I also believe that the family doctor no longer holds that post. That he was found wanting, shall we say.'

'Did Faun Moran ever come to your home?'

'She did, yes, with her sister when she was younger. And I believe she may have come once or twice since.'

'You believe? You can't be sure.'

'Chief Inspector Johnstone, from time to time people do visit my home and I don't keep count as to who and when.

Not as many as might visit your sister, of course, but then I'm not as sociable.'

'If you're not sociable then I'm surprised that you are here tonight.'

'The difference, Chief Inspector, is that I can walk away from this place anytime I like. If I have houseguests then I must entertain them. I'm expected to be present and attentive and frankly that soon becomes tiresome.' He drained his glass and then looked expectantly at Henry. 'Is there anything else?'

'As a matter of fact, there is. I won't keep you but I have two more questions. The first is did you ever write letters to Faun Moran?'

'Why would I write letters to her? She was the younger sister of a friend, that is all.'

'Would it be possible to have a sample of your handwriting, for the processes of elimination?'

Ben Caxton looked exasperated. He searched his pockets as though looking for a pen and paper. Henry obliged him with a notebook taken from his own pocket and a stub of pencil in a little silver holder. 'It's not a pen, I'm afraid, but it should do.'

'What would you like me to write?'

'Your name and address would do. That will serve double duty of saving me to look it up later.'

Caxton sighed but did as he was asked. 'You are becoming less entertaining by the minute,' he said. 'Now, what else do you want to ask me?'

'I believe there is a man called Victor Mullins in your employ.'

'No, Chief Inspector, there is not. Mr Mullins left me some time ago.'

'Oh, why is that?'

'Chief Inspector . . . Henry . . . Mullins was an employee. Employees sometimes choose to leave. I gave him good references and off he went. I believe he wanted to return home to Ireland, but as I haven't heard from him since he left, I have no idea where he is now.'

'Your house is quite remote and out of the way, I imagine

that might cause problems in terms of getting people to work there. Do you have a high turnover of staff?'

'What an odd question. As a matter of fact, I inherited most of the staff from my father, and they had been with him for many years. The only turnover, as you put it, is with the kitchen maids. Cook takes them on, trains them up and they usually find positions in other houses. As I'm sure you know, young girls don't want to go into service these days, but my household has a reputation for good treatment, and first-class training. They don't even have to pay for their uniforms. I happen to find it very offensive that a young woman might enter service, but it might take two full years to pay back the cost of her uniform and her training, such as it often is. The wages are egregious. Most domestic maids get little more than ten shillings a week. Don't you think that is disgraceful?'

The conversation had taken an unusual turn, Henry thought.

'I like to treat my staff well because that builds loyalty. My father thought the same and as I say we have members of staff that have been with the household for twenty or thirty years. My father disliked change, and I admit to similar feelings so the arrangement suits everybody. On retirement they know that they will have a cottage on one of the estates and a small pension. They are grateful for that, Chief Inspector.'

Someone spoke his name and Ben Caxton inclined his head towards Henry and then went off to join the young man who had called out to him. There was no backward glance towards Henry, who knew he'd been thoroughly dismissed. And he knew also that a message had been delivered. Don't poke about in my affairs, Ben Caxton was telling him. You won't find anybody to speak out against me. Which meant, Henry thought, that there must be something to speak out about. He glanced at the piece of paper on which was written the name and address of Ben Caxton and he realized immediately that the handwriting was quite different from that of the love letters.

'Damn,' Henry muttered. 'So if not him, who the hell wrote them?'

Vic

In a sixteenth-century trunk in an unused part of the house there were certain items that from time to time Vic felt the need to examine. Certain items of feminine clothing, a small mirror, a comb. A tiny but rather beautifully enamelled music box which when opened revealed a little bird which twittered and sang. A silver bracelet and a gold brooch. A cheap lipstick in a brass holder and a pretty hair clip shaped like a leaf.

He would remove these items and lay them out on the floor, stroking the little fox fur, the smooth silk of an evening dress, remembering and imagining, the memory of those women he had brought to this place before Faun had become Ben's latest chosen one. And then he would replace them, laying them carefully in the trunk before locking it, covering it once more with one of the ubiquitous dust sheets. It always seemed strange to Vic that his employer, though he saved these souvenirs, seemed not to need to look at them again. Ben's memory, it seemed, did not need refreshing.

It always seemed a shame to Vic that the house was not better used. Fires were lit occasionally in the unused wings just to keep the place aired and in the summer the windows were thrown open and the fresh air blew the stale winter away. The house was far too big for Ben Caxton, but Vic always knew that Ben would never be prepared to give it up.

FIFTEEN

Faun, December

Martha has agreed to take my letter. Oh God in heaven, I am so grateful. She will post my letter for me and Pat, I know that you will come and find me. You might not believe that your little sister is still alive but I know you will recognize my most terrible handwriting and you'll know that the letter comes from me. I don't have an envelope to give her or a stamp but she tells me she can manage to find those and will copy your address faithfully on to the envelope.

I am so grateful I could hug her, but I know if I tried she would skitter out of my reach like some scared little mouse. She cares for me and is kind, but she still thinks me mad.

I've been thinking about that book, Jane Eyre, you know the scene about the mad wife kept in the attic and how she sets fire to the house? I wish I could do that, but I'm not permitted a fire. When Martha is here she is permitted to bring an electric fire and the room is then warm for a little while, but he insists that she must take it away with her when she goes. She begged him to give me warmer covers for the bed and eventually he agreed, but the room is so cold that frost forms on the glass, curling like fern leaves. Do you remember when we were children and we would go up to the attic rooms to look at the frost ferns?

Pat, when you come and rescue me, I will want such a fire lit and I'll have a hot, hot bath and I will eat what I want and then sit in front of the fire and get warm and I'm going to sleep there, in front of the fire, curled up like a cat. Cold is misery, Pat. This is all misery.

He used to say that one day we would marry. We would elope like some ridiculous Regency couple and marry in secret and then reveal ourselves to our families as man and wife. As *a living, breathing wife. I used to listen to him and think what a grand story this would make but now it just seems so vile and so grotesque. Then he told me what he had done. About that poor girl they put in the car in my place. I told him that you would see through the trick but then he showed me the newspapers, the obituaries, the reports of my untimely death. How could you forgive me for putting you through my death? I wanted to be at the centre of my own, wonderful, precious, romantic story. I wanted to believe. I wanted to be loved by someone who told me I was the most precious soul he had ever met.*

Oh Pat, I was such a stupid little fool. Can you forgive me?

I know now that all he wants is to break me, body and soul. If you don't come for me, Pat, then I know I'm going to die. He'll kill me. He'll break me and then he'll kill me stone dead. As stone dead as that poor girl in the car.

Pat, what am I to do? Martha promises that she will send my letter. But what if she can't? What if you don't believe her? What if you come too late?

I'm so, so scared. I'm just so very frightened. I just don't know what to do.

Sunday 19 January

It took a little while before Pat came to the phone and Henry occupied himself by comparing the various samples of handwriting sitting on his desk to the letters signed with the florid R. From time to time he fancied that he saw a likeness in the way that a letter was formed or a T was crossed or in the swagger of a signature. But he knew there was nothing that was similar enough. He looked again at the handwriting of Ben Caxton, studying the way the letters were joined, the odd little breaks in words, as though there had been a moment of hesitation before writing the next syllable, and he wished that he had asked Ben Caxton to write a capital R or to note down something extracted from one of the letters, but the situation had not really been conducive to that.

All of this would be sent to the documents expert later in the hope that they might find some link that Henry could not see, but he held out little expectation.

Pat finally came to the phone. 'Good morning, Chief Inspector. I'm so sorry to have kept you. Now what can I do for you?'

'I happened to be speaking to Ben Caxton last night and he mentioned the two of you were once very close friends and that friendship led him to take a particular interest in your sister. I just wanted to ask you about this.'

There was a moment of silence on the other end of the telephone and then Pat said cautiously, 'Yes, we were close once. I suppose in a commonplace way we are still friendly. There were those, including my father, who would have liked the friendship to deepen into something more. It would have been a good match, I suppose, but I did not love him. If I'm being truthful I didn't even like him very much in the end. But I had no idea at first that he was in any way interested in Faun. It was only later, when other people commented on his interest, and then I looked more closely.'

'By his own admission he kept an eye on her. He talked about himself as a surrogate older brother.'

Again, that moment of silence. 'Do you suspect him of anything?'

That was a good question, Henry thought, and he didn't have an answer. 'I was speaking to him simply as someone who might have had dealings with your sister in the weeks before she disappeared. I've been speaking to a lot of people. My lists of friends and acquaintances are now very long indeed.'

'But you are not asking me about those others.'

That was a fair point. 'I may well ask about others, but for the moment I'm asking what you know about Ben Caxton. Other people commented on the fact that he was interested in your sister. The usual explanation was that he had been interested in you and so it did not seem so unnatural. He describes her as a child, a child who seemed lost and rather unhappy, and so he felt he had a duty to take on the older brother role.'

Pat laughed, but the sound was brittle and humourless. 'Oh yes, I imagine that would suit him very well.'

'Can I ask what you mean by that?'

'There are men who are charming, who engage and even seduce by the charm. And once you are in their thrall they become more and more possessive of what you do and what you say and what you think. How you dress and who you choose to see. I could imagine that being trapped in a marriage with a man like that would be difficult in the extreme, and this is why, even though Ben Caxton asked me to be his wife, I refused. My father was not pleased. He and Ben had business deals they wanted to move forward, and after I rejected him these business deals were taken off the table. My father, I believe, lost some money. Shortly after that I met my husband, fell in love, married and moved away from my father's house. Now I rarely even visit. Does that begin to answer your question, Chief Inspector?'

'It does, thank you, Mrs Clifford, Pat, though it would have been helpful to have known this before. Tell me, did you meet a man called Victor Mullins when you were still on close terms with Mr Caxton?'

'Vic – yes, it would be hard not to meet Vic. Technically Ben was Vic's employer but they behaved more like equals, more like friends. They seem to have a shared language, a shared connection that I didn't always understand, but I suppose that's because Vic was the one who brought him back from the war and looked after him.'

'Brought him back?'

'Ben was seriously wounded, as no doubt you know. He was shipped to a field hospital and his father was notified that he might not survive. His father, having the money and resources to do so, moved heaven and earth to have his son collected and brought back to England and Vic was the man who did that. He was only young, but as an Irish citizen was not compelled to join the war. He was, I believe, a stockman on the agricultural part of the estate for old Mr Caxton and by all accounts doing so very well and Mr Caxton took a fancy to him, decided that he would promote him and give him a better position. Anyway, he apparently volunteered to go to France and fetch the young master home and that's what he did. It can't have been easy, and it can't have been easy keeping

Ben alive on that return journey. I suppose the two of them became friends.'

'And is this Vic of a similar type to Ben Caxton?'

'He can be as controlling, I think, but less obviously so. I didn't know him well, Henry. He was just someone that was always there ready to do Ben's bidding. If I was visiting the house it was often Vic who was sent to fetch me. I remember I was discouraged from driving my own car there, so I was dependent on Vic or Ben if I wanted to leave. At first it seemed like a courtesy and then it seemed irritating, and then it seemed more than that. It was as though even in this simple little instance Ben wanted to know where I was and that I couldn't leave and that I didn't have my independence. Growing up with someone like my father, I've come to value my independence enormously.'

'I can understand that,' Henry told her honestly.

'I was old enough, Inspector . . . no, mature enough is probably a better way to put it, to know that I didn't like what was going on and that I must stand my ground, but Faun was not like me. Since our mother died Faun had been a lost soul. She had no one to guide her. I did my best but I had married and moved away so it became much more difficult for her. I offered her a home with us, told her she could come and stay until she had money of her own, but she seemed intent on living in London, and on living her own life. I was just glad that she was away from my father's house, but it seems I should have taken better care of her.'

'You could not have known.'

'Oh, but I should have known. I did know how wilful she was and I did know that if anybody warned Faun away from anything that would be the direction she would take. I should have understood that better and acted upon it.'

'And did you warn her away from Ben Caxton?'

Pat laughed bitterly. 'Initially I warned her away from Victor Mullins,' she said. 'She told me she'd seen him box and I was appalled. I know respectable women go to see boxing matches, but I'm not convinced it is a place for a girl of eighteen as she would have been. She wouldn't tell me who had taken her, but from what you've told me it was obviously Ben Caxton. She talked about Victor as being so alive, animalistic but also intelligent. Essentially I think she just had a pash, a girlish crush, and it would have died down and passed over as these things do, but it seems it led her into trouble.'

'I have no proof of that; I have no solid proof against anybody or relating to anything just now.'

'But your instincts tell you that Ben Caxton was involved in my sister's death.'

'The evidence tells me that the accident was no accident, that the girl in the car was killed before she was placed there and set alight, which is a small mercy as I'm sure you'll agree. That your sister may not have been complicit in the staging of this accident but she was almost certainly present. The evidence suggests that Mal Everson was innocent in all of this. It's not possible to know if something was put into his drink but it is likely, and it's also likely he wasn't driving and knew nothing about the other girl. Beyond that there is very little to say.

'Pat, did your sister ever talk about receiving love letters from somebody with the initial R?'

'Love letters? No, and who is R?'

'We don't know. Of course R may be a subterfuge, a misdirection. The letters have no return address and are signed only with the initial. If I have one sent over to you, could you look at it and see if you recognize the handwriting or anything else about it?'

'Certainly. Should I also ask Violet? She's staying with us for a little time. She had a most enormous argument with her father when she got home from seeing Mal. He will calm down – Everson Senior is not a bad sort, but he does have peculiar ideas about the place of women and that they should not get involved in the affairs of men. Anything to do with business or unpleasantness he sees in exactly that way. I think he just wants to protect her, but is going the wrong way about it.'

'If you could ask Miss Everson that would be most helpful,' Henry told her.

Ben

She had written many letters, in that rounded, schoolroom, undeveloped hand of hers, full of gushing and ill-considered emotions. She adored him, he was the perfect man, she wanted nothing more than to be with him and his letters filled with her with joy.

Not much joy in the end, Ben thought and his lips twisted into a grimace.

He twisted the letter he held into a spill and used it to light his cigarette, holding the tip in the fire until it caught. Then he dropped the paper into the flames and watched it burn. That was the last of them, infantile emotions reduced to ash and, as he prodded them with the poker, disappearing into the wood ash and the coal dust beneath.

He would have preferred Pat. As his wife there would have been some permanence to the relationship and he would have enjoyed the challenge of breaking a woman like that. Faun had offered no such challenge. She had thrown herself in his direction and she had been fun for a time.

The problem was, Ben acknowledged, he was so easily bored.

SIXTEEN

Mickey Hitchens had had a busy day, dividing his time between the records of Companies House and various newspaper archives. Late that afternoon he laid his findings on Henry's desk, then sat down opposite to explain.

'You were correct in your guess – Ben Caxton and Caius Moran were indeed partners of record for some eighteen months, a relationship that formally ended just over four years ago. The business, Titus Imports, had more or less finished trading about a year before that. There were various financial and legal threads to disentangle, which I don't begin to understand, but which I don't think are relevant to us.'

'That would fit with what Pat told me,' Henry said, 'that her father seemed to envisage some kind of personal and business alliance, and it would have suited him had Pat married Ben Caxton and their businesses come together in a more formal kind of way. Did the end come amicably?'

'It would seem not, from the number of solicitors' letters flying back and forth. I can't access everything, of course, not without a proper warrant. I went there today effectively as a member of the general public and then had an interesting little discussion with one of the clerks, who explained matters to me in a very off-the-record way. But of course, what I have from him is inference rather than evidence and if you wish to dig deeper then we will need to get the experts involved.'

'If that becomes necessary then that's what we'll do, but for the moment what we need is an overview of their business dealings. And how have the respective businesses been impacted by the Wall Street crash and the stock market collapse?'

'It's a matter of record that both took hits, but then Caxton seems to be recovering. His investments were more widely

spread and more cautious, but Moran lost a packet when
Wall Street went down. He had invested heavily in American
securities and though he is now putting on a brave face, he is
also quietly selling stocks and property and not for the full
market value.'

'And Caxton?'

'As I say, seems to be recovering. He sold a number of
assets in June last year, before the problems really started, and
liquidated several of his holdings. It's as though he saw trouble
coming. By all accounts he is a shrewd businessman and
prefers businesses where the initial investments are not
great and the turnarounds are swift. He's been involved in
importing and exporting, mostly fine art and jewellery and has
a gallery in London. He also keeps the agricultural traditions
going, it seems these were the foundation of his family's wealth
and old Mr Caxton was well thought of as a man who actually
knew what he was talking about when it came to breeding
sheep and cattle.'

'And what have you discovered about Ben Caxton, other
than his business dealings?'

'I did as you suggested and perused the society pages and
announcements for the last decade. Truthfully we should have
persuaded your Cynthia to do that; she'd have been a dab hand
at it. I scarcely knew where to look at first, but you might be
interested to know that Ben Caxton has been engaged on no
less than three occasions. The final time to Pat Moran.'

'She was actually engaged to him? She didn't tell me that.'

'It was short-lived,' Mickey said. 'If it actually happened
at all. From what I can gather Caxton posted the announce-
ment. Pat rather publicly refuted it. The whole thing was passed
off as a prank to save too much embarrassment; you remember
there was a fad, a few summers ago, for mock weddings and
phony engagements and general shenanigans. I never did like
practical jokes, Henry. But it seems everyone chose to accept
this as an explanation and no more was said.'

'Though I can't imagine Caius Moran seeing the funny
side.'

'Indeed, no.'

'You said Caxton had been engaged before. Twice before?'

'And each time he came out of the situation advantageously. The first was to a widow by the name of Nora Oldman. She was at that time only thirty-three years old and the sole beneficiary of her late husband's estate. Six months after his death she became involved with Mr Caxton and engaged three months after that. The newspapers reported it as a whirlwind romance and the wedding was set for December the twenty-seventh 1923. It seems that Mrs Oldman wanted everything settled legally before she took the plunge and she signed her will a month after the engagement, leaving everything to Ben Caxton. Then she drove her car off the road and into a frozen dyke, somewhere in the Cambridgeshire Fens two days before Christmas. The police report suggests black ice.'

'Convenient,' Henry said.

'But as likely to be an accident as it is to be foul play. There was no suggestion of anything untoward and though her relatives challenged it, the will was carefully drawn up and witnessed and their opposition got them nowhere.'

'And the second engagement?'

'To Miss Julia Farnham in 1926. She was twenty-eight at the time and her parents had recently died. She was left in charge of the family acres which, as it happened, adjoined farmland owned by the Caxton family. She was known to suffer from depression and it seemed even an engagement to the eligible Mr Caxton was insufficient cure for that malady. The poor woman took an "accidental" overdose of her sleeping draft and died, a month before the marriage was supposed to take place. Caxton got the land. He'd apparently bought it from her for a pittance under the pretext that it would soon be their joint land through the marriage.'

'In which case why not wait for the wedding? Her property would have been his property from the moment they signed the register, so he could have saved even that pittance of a payment.'

'It's a question a number of people, including the local newspaper editor, seem to have asked. Caxton bought the local paper and sacked the editor and senior staff. He is not a man who likes to be crossed.'

'Somewhat like Caius Moran, then. Pat had a lucky escape – from both of them.'

'But the younger daughter still had money coming to her,' Mickey said. 'From what her sister told us, she would have come into her fortune, from her mother's trust, when she was twenty-five.'

'That's a long time ahead when you are only nineteen.'

'It is, but aren't these trusts often broken if marriage comes first? What if Faun Moran would come into her money when she married?'

'What makes you think that is the case?'

'Because of something her older sister said. Pat Moran, as she was, has only just turned twenty-five. She was married at twenty-one and from what she inferred – unless I misunderstood – she had already received her legacy before she reached the age of twenty-five.'

Henry pulled the telephone towards him and asked for a call to be placed to Pat Clifford. She was surprised to hear from him twice in two days.

'Yes, you are quite right,' Pat told him. 'I came into my money when I was twenty-one, just after my marriage. My father wasn't happy about it, but our mother's family had ensured that he could do nothing about it. That was always a sore point with our father, that our maternal grandfather had made this provision before our mother married. When we were all born some kind of codicil was added that divided the money from her family's estate equally between us. Grandfather died a few years ago and big chunks of the estate went in death duties, of course, but that trust fund was separate and not affected, I suppose because it had been set up so long ago.'

Henry thanked her and then asked, 'What do you know about Titus Imports? Your father and Ben Caxton seem to have been directors of that company for a short while.'

'Titus Imports,' she said thoughtfully. 'Was that the diamond mining thing?'

'Diamond mining?' Henry looked at Mickey, who shrugged. 'I don't know. It ended around the time that your engagement to Ben Caxton was announced.'

'Oh,' she said. 'That. He had no right to make that kind of

assumption. He told me that my father had suggested it to him, that my father implied I'd not be able to say no if he'd already announced it. Well, he was wrong about that. There was hell to pay; my father told me I'd not get another penny out of him unless I agreed to the wedding. I went off to stay with my great aunt. My mother's Aunt Laura, until things cooled down. Aunt Laura was a suffragette, so you can guess whose side she was on!'

'A useful ally,' Henry agreed, thinking that this probably explained a lot about Pat. Perhaps Faun should have been sent to stay with Aunt Laura, if she was still around.

'Do you think he's taken some kind of revenge because of a broken engagement that never was?' Pat asked quietly. 'Would Ben Caxton do that?'

'I couldn't say,' Henry told her, 'but we will find out. I promise you that.'

He replaced the receiver and relayed to Mickey those parts of the conversation that he had missed.

Mickey sat back in his chair, hands crossed over his waistcoat and surveyed his boss thoughtfully. 'He's our man, I'm certain of it.'

'But our man for what? For arranging the accident that almost certainly wasn't an accident? For killing Faun Moran and that other poor scrap of a girl? For what?'

'All or any of the above,' Mickey said confidently.

'So how do we prove that? He's a slippery customer and a rich one. A man with friends and influence and you know how much that complicates things.'

'And we've never yet let that stop us before,' Mickey told him. 'So we won't this time.'

SEVENTEEN

They were about to leave for the evening when a message came for Henry that someone called Victor Mullins had come to the reception looking for him and was saying that he wanted to talk about Faun Moran.

'The plot thickens,' Mickey said.

His first sight of Vic Mullins impressed upon Henry that the witnesses who had seen him on the beach had been correct. This was an uncommonly big man, both in height and breadth and Henry could understand why they had felt intimidated.

'I've come to confess,' Mullins said.

'Confess to what?' Henry asked him.

A slow smile spread across Mullins' face. 'To putting the body on the beach,' he said. 'And maybe one or two other things.'

They took him into an interview room and Henry sat down opposite Mullins, Mickey a little to the side, with his notepad and pen. The oddness of the situation had struck them both, as had the confidence and swagger of Vic Mullins when they had taken him upstairs and settled down in this bare, utilitarian space with its scrubbed wooden table and uncomfortable chairs.

'Perhaps you should start at the beginning,' Henry said.

'That depends where you think the beginning should be.'

It was very clear, Henry thought, that this man was enjoying himself. Henry was not prepared to indulge him. 'January the fifth,' he said. 'Sunday. You were seen on Bournemouth beach carrying the body of a young woman. The body of Miss Faun Moran. You waited until you were noticed and then you laid her body on the shingle and you walked away.'

Mullins nodded, clearly unconcerned. 'That's about the size of it, yes.'

'Her neck was broken.'

'It was.'

'And were you responsible for her death?'

'I was not.'

This was becoming irritating, Henry thought. 'And so how did she die?'

'She slipped, she fell, she hit her head and her neck broke. Sad, but that's the way things go sometimes. She was an unfortunate young woman all round, was young Miss Moran. You couldn't help but feel sorry for her. For what it's worth, I liked her very much. I think she made some bad judgements, but she didn't deserve to die, not even by accident.'

'And where was this and how did you come to be there?'

Mullins grinned, a self-satisfied grin, a suggestive grin, Henry thought. He waited.

'I wasn't there when it happened. I was just charged with taking the body, making sure that she was seen and found.'

'Then why not take her back to her family?'

'Ah yes, that would have been the most sensible idea. I walk up to Caius Moran's door and I drop her on the doorstep and tell him, here's your kid back. Fat chance I'd have had of getting away after that. Moran would have had me shot!'

'And yet you walk into Scotland Yard and you give yourself up.'

Mullins leaned across the table and stared into Henry's eyes and said, 'I've got a conscience. Things happened to this young lady that I've got a conscience about. That's why I wanted her found, you see. That's why I waited until those people saw me, and then I put her down and I walked off when I was sure that they would take care of her.'

Henry blinked. He felt as though he was in some kind of surreal play. 'So who told you to dispose of the body? Did they tell you to dump her on a beach?'

'Not exactly. Mad as hell when I told him what I'd done.'

'Who was?'

'My employer.'

'And that would be?'

'Don't play games, Chief Inspector. You know who it is.'

'Mr Caxton told me that you were no longer in his employ.'
It was the first time Mickey had spoken. Mullins turned to
look at him.

'Well, he lied about that, didn't he?'

'And why would Mr Caxton be in possession of Miss
Moran's body? Did he kill her?'

Mullins frowned. 'I told you it was an accident.'

'An accident you said you did not witness.'

'I was there just after. He called me in, said she'd
slipped in the bathroom on the tiles, fallen and hit her head
against the bath and the blow twisted her neck and she was
dead.'

'And how is it that Mr Caxton was present?'

'Ah now, that is difficult. Mr Caxton has been good to me.
His father was good to me before that, but Mr Caxton does
not always behave like a gentleman should behave, at
least not where the young ladies are concerned. You have to
understand, Miss Moran was in a bit of a pickle and Mr Caxton
helped her out.' He paused as though considering what to say
next but seemed in no hurry to work it out.

'Miss Moran was believed to have died in June of last year,
so who was the young woman in the car? What happened
when the car went off the road? Where has Miss Moran been
for these last months?'

'Well, you have a number of questions there,' Mullins told
him. 'I don't know the identity of the young woman in the
car. Why should I? I know only that Miss Moran was unhappy
and did not want to be at home. That her father was pressuring
her to do something she did not want to do and she came to
Mr Caxton for help, seeing as how he'd been a close friend
of her older sister.'

'And why did she not go to her sister for help?'

'I suppose because she thought her sister would tell their
father where she was, or her sister's husband would.' He sat
back, evidently relaxed, and said, 'The idea, as I understand
it, was that she would lie low for a while and then when she
and Mr Caxton had tied the knot she would reappear, a married
woman, no longer under Daddy's thumb and all would be
sweetness and light.'

'But then she had an accident and she died.'

'You understand the situation perfectly.'

'I don't actually think I do. Perhaps you'd explain to me what the car crash had to do with this and why a young woman like Faun Moran, who by all accounts is a very pleasant sort, would put her family through so much anguish. And what do you mean by Miss Moran and Mr Caxton intending to tie the knot?'

'A pleasant sort. Is that what you think? A pleasant young woman who colluded in staging her own death.'

Henry had the distinct impression that he was being played, but he knew he had to humour this man if he had any hope of getting to the truth. 'Staging her own death?'

'The car crash. You see, what happened was my boss gave us something to slip into that young man's drink so that he would go woozy, pass out, and then he said he would drive them to where the crash was going to be, tip the car over the side, chuck that young bloke's body down the hill, so everybody would assume he'd been in the car and then thrown out. Then they'd make like it was Faun's body in the car, burned up in the fire. I'd follow on in Ben's car and pick them both up.'

'And you are claiming that she colluded in all of this?'

'Of course she did. The girl liked a bit of an adventure. My boss persuaded her that nobody would be hurt by this, and sooner or later she could come out of hiding and everybody would be just so relieved she was still alive, and married, of course, that they'd forgive her. They'd go to Scotland to be wed, I expect. No one gives a damn up there. Job done.'

'And the girl in the car?'

'Dead already so what does it matter?'

'It would matter to her family.'

'The family won't know about it, will they? What they don't know can't hurt.'

'There is a family somewhere missing a daughter. Of course it matters.'

'Well, I know nothing about that. I don't know who she was or where he got her from, or who helped him obtain a body. But it sure as hell wasn't me. I only found out about all this after the event, you understand that.'

'Rather you only found out that Faun was dead after that happened and then you helped your boss cover it up.'

'Quite so. I admit to helping get her dressed and taking her to the beach, which is not what my boss intended at all.'

'And what did he intend?'

'Well, he reckoned least said soonest mended, in a manner of speaking. The family already believed that she was dead and gone, so why would they be bothered? He told me to bury her and have done with it.'

'And so you dressed her in a very expensive gown, combed her hair and decorated it with a headband. That seems unlikely if you are going to bury the body.'

'But that wasn't what I intended, was it, but I wasn't going to tell him that.'

'You said you helped to get her dressed,' Mickey interrupted. 'So who did you help? Your boss?'

'No, he didn't want anything to do with it. Like I say, I had a conscience. She was a respectable young woman and needed to go back to her family.'

'And so who helped get her dressed?'

'What does it matter?'

'And why did you dress her in somebody else's clothes?' Mickey wanted to know.

It was only a second, but Henry saw that Mullins was momentarily disconcerted.

'The shoes were too big,' Mickey continued, 'the under-clothes too big, the dress several sizes too large. Though you might be forgiven for not realizing that as the heavy beading would have made it hang closer to her body, even though the size was wrong. The style anyway is meant to be loose. But the rest, that was careless, especially the shoes. Which leads me to another question. Who did those clothes belong to?'

'How the hell should I know?' For the first time Vic Mullins was clearly disconcerted.

'And you admit to nothing else, just to dumping the body on the beach?'

'I did not *dump* the body!' Vic was suddenly on his feet. 'I laid her where she would be seen and found.'

'Sit down, Mr Mullins, or do I have to get the constables to make you?'

Vic's eyes narrowed dangerously, but he resumed his seat. 'I came here to confess to taking the body and making sure that she was seen. Maybe you'd rather I dumped her in some shallow grave somewhere.'

'Why didn't you?'

'I told you. I've got a conscience.' He was on his feet again. 'I've had enough of this,' he said. 'I'm leaving.'

'No, you're not,' Henry told him.

'I've done nothing wrong.'

'We'll start with preventing a proper burial,' Henry said, 'and we'll take it from there.'

Mickey got to his feet and opened the interview room door. Two constables entered and Henry ordered them to escort Mullins to a cell. 'You can't do this,' Vic protested. 'I did nothing wrong,' But Henry got the distinct impression that Mullins felt himself on safe ground now. That detention was expected and did not trouble him overmuch. He still had the strangest impression that Mullins was enjoying himself; that he was still controlling the situation – or thought he was.

Mullins paused in the doorway. 'I got the dress from a chest he keeps in the small ballroom. He reckons it's old, the chest – sixteenth century, carved oak or some such. It's a room that don't get used any more in the locked-up part of the house. You look in there. You'll find other things. Things from other women. He's completely off his head – everyone knows that. Has been since the war. Thinks he can get away with anything and he doesn't give a damn who he hurts in the process, I'll tell you that for nothing.'

'Where in the house do you claim Faun Moran was kept all this time?' Mickey asked him but Mullins just scowled and shook his head. 'You find that trunk,' he said. 'That's all I'm saying now.'

'So, what do we make of all that?' Henry asked when they had adjourned back to the office.

'He's lying to us, but about what? Is Ben Caxton at the back of this . . . was the girl directly involved? What was Mullins' part in all of this? And, more importantly, do you think we'll get a warrant to search the Caxton place?'

Henry drew the necessary forms across the desk and set to work. 'We can but try,' he said. 'Best get a message to Belle that you might be late tonight.'

EIGHTEEN

Tuesday 21 January

No warrant, Henry had been told. What evidence did he have? Just some cock and bull story told by a disaffected ex-employee.

'He admits to leaving the body on the beach,' he told the assistant commissioner.

'So charge him – suspicion of murder. Whatever else you can make stick. Ask yourself, would a man like Mr Caxton involve himself in something as bizarre as this?'

'The fact remains that it was not Faun Moran's body in that car.'

'So go and question Everson about it. Perhaps some other young woman tagged along. Perhaps that's just another fact he can claim not to recall.'

Henry had given up. The assistant commissioner had been adamant. There was nothing to support the issuing of a search warrant.

'Because Ben Caxton is such a fine upstanding citizen,' Henry complained to Mickey.

'So are we going to pay him a visit anyway?'

'Damn right we are.'

Cynthia and her husband were still in London and Henry had arranged to borrow their car so they arrived at Ben Caxton's place in some style. It had occurred to Mickey that he might not be home, but he had said nothing as Henry was not in the mood to hear and Mickey comforted himself with the thought that they could at least question the servants even if the master was away.

Ben Caxton's house was impressive. It was large in front and clad with pale stone that looked ghostly on a winter's day. It had drizzled with rain all morning and the sky was overcast and heavy and miserable.

The long driveway curved as they drew close to the house and Mickey could see that the main building was extended into two long wings. Another block behind presumably housed stables although somehow this did not look like a place where people rode or walked in the grounds or even enjoyed themselves very much. It had a melancholy air to it, Mickey thought, although it had undoubtedly once been an impressive pile.

The door was opened to them by an elderly man who seemed a little shocked by their presence, as though spontaneous visitors were not commonplace. He had just asked them to wait in the hall when a man's voice called out from above.

'Henry, what are you doing here? Or are you here as Chief Inspector Johnstone today?'

Mickey looked up. Ben Caxton stood on the landing, leaning over the balustrade and looking down at them, his expression curious and, Mickey thought, a little amused.

'I saw the car arrive and I couldn't think who you might be. I'm assuming it's not police issue? I doubt the police could afford such a decent vehicle.'

'Most definitely not,' Henry agreed. In contrast to Caxton's outward friendliness Henry's tone was flat. Mickey felt himself tense and guessed that this next scene was not going to be played out with any level of subtlety or conciliation.

'So it's official business then. Come along up. There's a fire lit in my study – we'll be more comfortable there.'

Obediently they climbed the stairs to where Caxton was waiting and followed him into a room at the front of the house. Mickey looked about with interest. The walls were lined with books. Books that looked well-thumbed and appreciated, not the sort procured by the yard, just for effect. A large desk stood off to one side and a comfortable looking sofa had been placed by the window with a small table close by on which rested a book and a glass.

He wondered what their host had been reading.

Caxton must have registered his curiosity because he said, 'It's a treatise on microscopy that was published in 1667.'

Mickey's interest was piqued further. 'Robert Hooke's *Micrographia*? I have a very tatty but much-loved copy that my wife found in a second-hand bookshop. Microscopy is a big interest of mine, though my microscope is not such a grand instrument as yours.' He had noticed on a table by the window a rather smart brass microscope and an extensive selection of slides in a box.

'May I see?'

'Of course. Please do. It's good to meet a fellow enthusiast.'

Henry's irritation was palpable. 'We did not come here to talk about slides and old books,' he said impatiently.

Mickey and Caxton exchanged a look. Caxton shrugged. 'Your superior has spoken,' he said, 'but Henry, Chief Inspector, I'm sure it won't take both of you to question me, so perhaps your sergeant could have a moment or two to review my handiwork.'

The pride in his voice was unmistakable. 'You mount your own slides?' Mickey asked.

'Of course, I don't believe in doing half a job. If you are to do a thing, then it should be done properly.'

On the drive here they had discussed strategy. Henry was in a temper, and Mickey knew that he would be unlikely to cool down even by the end of the lengthy drive. His annoyance and impatience, not having to be faked, would play its part in this interview. Mickey's role had been less certain but it seemed that he had found it now. The conversation was interrupted by a polite knock, followed by the elderly retainer they had met on arrival entering with a tray. He placed this down on a stand and asked if anything further might be required. Mickey took the opportunity to move across to the microscope and slides. He caught Caxton's expression as he saw this; he looked, Mickey thought, like a cat who'd got the cream, a cat whose policy was also to divide and conquer, Mickey added to himself, quite enjoying the mixed proverbs. His pleasure at examining the scientific instrument did not have to be feigned. He'd not lied when he avowed an interest in the subject.

'It's a fine instrument,' he said, 'by Negretti and Zambra.'

'I don't care how fine it is, Sergeant,' Henry snapped. 'That is not what we came here for.'

The look of annoyance on Caxton's face was unmistakable.

He's easily rattled, then, Mickey thought. For all his slickness.

Obediently, Mickey came back to where his boss was standing and withdrew his notebook, murmuring what might be construed as an apology.

'So what did you come here for, Chief Inspector?' Caxton asked coldly.

'We had a visit, yesterday, from an employee of yours. One Mr Victor Mullins—'

'Who, I told you when we met before, is no longer in my service.'

'He tells me otherwise. He also directly implicates you in the car crash that injured Mr Malcolm Everson and killed an unknown woman that everyone believed at the time was Miss Faun Moran.'

'That's absurd. Mullins is a fantasist. What am I supposed to have done?'

'He also states that you were witness to the events that did eventually cost Miss Moran her life and that you commissioned him to dispose of the body.'

Caxton stared in disbelief and then he began to laugh. 'Oh, Henry,' he said. 'Do you honestly believe any of that? Look, I dismissed Mullins because he was getting to be a liability. He caused trouble with the staff. He couldn't seem to leave the younger women alone and he had no discretion about it either. He seemed to think that because my father and I both showed him favour he could get away with anything he liked. Mullins is a liar and a thief and a cad and I don't want a man like him about the place.'

'He seemed very certain of his facts.'

'His facts? What facts?'

Henry gestured to Mickey who opened his notebook and relayed all that Vic Mullins had told them the evening before. By the end of it Ben Caxton was laughing harder and, Mickey guessed, Henry did not have to feign discomfort.

'I'll tell you what, Henry,' Caxton said, 'let me call my secretary and I'll prove to you that Victor Mullins is a liar.'

Caxton tugged gently on an embroidered bell pull and they sat in silence until a maid arrived, maintained the silence while she went to fetch the secretary. Mickey took the opportunity to scrutinize the shelves of books, trying not to be obvious in his desire to take a closer look. He knew that Caxton noticed anyway and that Henry did too, but the chief inspector sat still as stone and looked at neither Mickey nor their host.

The secretary was also an older man. Mickey remembered what Caxton had told Henry about inheriting most of the staff and guessed that this was part of that legacy.

'Clarke, can you find the diary entries for January of this year and . . . what was the date of the party?'

Mickey told him.

'Ah yes. And the pay books, please. I could find them myself,' he added as Clarke opened a doorway in one of the bookcases and went through into a little anteroom, 'but Clarke will lay hands on them so much more quickly.'

Silence again while they waited, then the books were brought. Caxton flipped through pages of an account book. 'Here, you see, I struck his name from the payments. My accountant would verify this, should you ask him. Mr Mullins was paid on the quarter days, as are all of my employees. As are my creditors and merchants.'

He dropped the book on the floor at Henry's feet. Henry made no move to pick it up.

'And here, the date of the party last year. Mullins and I were in Yorkshire. I was attending a funeral, an old friend of my fathers. We then spent a few days at a hotel and spent time walking and fishing in the Ribble Valley. There's some fine fishing up that way if you've a mind. Clarke will supply you with the details. And in early January of this year I was again away from home. I had been invited to spend the whole of the festive season with friends. The Philpots, a family who reside in Kent. I had arrived on Christmas Eve and remained until twelfth night, isn't that right, Clarke?'

Clarke nodded. 'As you do most years, sir.'

'Philpot and I were at school together, we've been friends ever since. Clarke will provide you with what details you might need. Where Mullins was, I've no idea, he'd left my employ by then. But I can assure you I was nowhere near Miss Moran, dead or alive.'

He rose. 'Now if that's all?'

'There was another thing,' Mickey said tentatively, glancing at his boss and then back to his notebook. 'Mullins said there was a box of stuff we should take a look at.'

'A box of stuff, Sergeant. What box? What stuff?'

Mickey peered closely at what he had written. 'A sixteenth-century carved chest that you keep in an unused part of the house. He said there would be evidence in it.'

'Evidence. Evidence of what?'

Mickey shrugged. 'I'm not sure, sir.'

'Oh, for Pete's sake. All right, Sergeant, I know the chest he must be referring to. Clarke, kindly find the addresses Chief Inspector Johnstone requires and then be so good as to show Sergeant Hitchens the old oak chest in the small ballroom.'

He glanced at his watch. 'Now, if that's all, gentlemen, I have better things to do with my time.'

Caxton left, Clarke disappeared once more into the ante-room and Henry shifted position so he could watch as Clarke carefully inscribed both names and addresses on a sheet of blue writing paper. Mickey took the opportunity to examine the bookcase at the opposite end of the room that mirrored the entrance to the little office. The latch was very hard to see, concealed inside the frame and opened by inserting a finger into a small, oval aperture. Mickey's little finger would just fit, he lifted the latch, met resistance. Some kind of lock, he supposed.

The idea of secret rooms appealed.

Clarke came back to find both visitors standing in the centre of the room. He handed Henry the sheet of paper. 'I'll take you two gentlemen to the small ballroom,' he said.

'Sergeant, you go. I propose to wait in the car.' Henry's tone was icy.

'He doesn't like not getting his own way,' Mickey muttered as they watched Henry march back down the stairs.

'None of them ever do,' Clarke agreed.

He led Mickey across the landing and through a small door. A spiral staircase led downward. 'This is the quickest route,' Clarke said. 'Otherwise it's back down and through the dining room, and into the east wing through the long gallery. And all of that's locked up just now so I'd have to fetch the keys. The master keeps the small staircase unlocked because it's easier for the servants to come up and down without disturbing him.'

'This place is a maze,' Mickey said. 'You have a long gallery? I thought this house would be the wrong date for something like that?'

'Oh, parts of the house go back to the 1500s. You'd never know it from the outside, of course, successive generations of Caxtons built on and up and sideways and every which way. But it is at least a house of character.'

'Do you have any priest holes here?' Mickey asked eagerly.

'There are two. The second was only discovered in the late Mr Caxton's time. It's off the long gallery but it's quite small and insignificant as these things go.'

'I can imagine the games of hide and seek this house must have seen over the years.' Mickey's tone was wistful.

'Oh yes, indeed. In old Mr Caxton's younger days, but young Mr Caxton doesn't like the bother of big house parties.'

Mickey was not sure if Clarke was saddened by that or relieved. If Clarke and the butler were examples of the staff, Mickey thought, they'd be more inclined to want to doze the afternoon away in a fireside chair than to prepare for guests on a grand scale.

The narrow staircase emerged into a narrow corridor. Mickey heard sounds that sounded like food preparation and a briefly opened door released the scent of cake. So that way to the right led to the kitchen. They went left, emerging from another small door into a very large room that was, according to Clarke, the grand ballroom. It was now an empty space, the polished floor mostly concealed beneath drop cloths and the pier glasses covered by dust sheets.

Another door, a small dining room and a chamber off and then a corridor and another entrance into, 'the small ballroom,' Clarke announced. 'The box you want is, I think, over there.'

This space was used for storage, Mickey assumed. A mountain of furniture had been covered with dust sheets and a row of tea chests stood against one wall. Clarke uncovered what he thought might be what Mickey was looking for but that too was just a tea chest. They rummaged for a while and eventually found the oak six-panelled box under yet another dust sheet. The key was in the lock; Mickey turned it. Inside there was only an elaborate lock and a lot of empty space.

Clarke, peering over Mickey's shoulder, huffed in disappointment. 'Nothing there,' he said. 'Not even moths.'

He stepped back to give Mickey space to get up and did not notice as Mickey scooped something from the corner of the chest.

'Empty,' he agreed. 'But it's a lovely old chest. What a beautiful lock and as smooth as it must have been back in the day.'

'Indeed it is,' Clarke said. 'Now I'm going to take you out by the rear entrance, you'll have to walk around the side of the house. I hope you don't mind that?'

Mickey said that he did not.

Clarke led him out through the small ballroom and into what he guessed must have once served as a cloakroom or perhaps small withdrawing room. Then down a service corridor and out through a door at the rear of the house, facing the stables Mickey had glimpsed as they drove up. Clarke gave him directions and then closed the door.

Mickey paused for a moment before following the line of the house around to the front drive. He took out a clean handkerchief and wiped fresh oil from his hand. Then from where he had pressed it beneath his thumbnail, a tiny scrap of thread and a single bead. These he folded into a twist of paper torn from his notebook.

It could have come from anywhere, but Mickey would be willing to bet his pension that it would match the beading used on the dress Faun Moran had been wearing when her body had been left on Bournemouth beach.

From an upstairs window Ben Caxton watched Mickey round the corner of the house and make his way back to the car. Clarke knocked gently on the door. 'I showed him the box, sir, though it did take us a while to find it. Someone had moved it into the far corner instead of where it had been beneath the window.'

'Things get moved all the time,' Ben said vaguely, though

that was not exactly true. There were pieces of old furniture stored in that room that had been there for the best part of the last decade.

'Yes, sir,' Clarke said and removed himself, as silently as ever.

The car drove away and Caxton found he was remembering another car arriving unexpectedly, this time on a rainy, treacherous night. Faun had driven too fast along the lane and skidded to a halt in front of the house. He had heard the car arrive and then heard Vic's voice in the hall, talking to the girl.

She had been distraught. Another argument with her father had led to her storming from the house and she had come here. To him. To the man she counted as her dearest friend. The man she wanted to be far more than that.

You're too young for me, he had told her. Your father doesn't like me at all. He told you that.

All reasons for her to want him even more.

He said the most hateful things. That you are a cheat and a liar and cost him money and reputation when you reneged on some business deal or other. But I don't care about any of that. I just want to be with you.

It's all true, my dear.

No, no, it's not, I won't believe anything like that of you. I know you and I know what you truly are.

No, he had told her. No, you don't.

In the end she had understood and in the end she had hated him for it. Wanted to run from him as she had once run from her father. The trouble was, he thought, as he saw Henry Johnstone's vehicle round the bend and disappear, by then the world had thought her dead and buried so she had nowhere left to run and no one left to care if she tried.

Vic

Lying on his back on the too-short, too-narrow bench in the small and dimly lit police cell, Vic remembered.

He had told the truth – he had no idea who the dead girl was but then neither had the mortuary. She was an unknown, picked up off the street after a collision with a car. It had taken him nearly a month to find the right body; right height and weight and approximate build, but it was simply happenstance that she'd not had anything with her to confirm identity.

The mortuary attendant he had bribed to keep him informed told him that if she'd had a handbag then it had not been handed in. In all likelihood someone had picked it up at the scene of the collision and either kept it or, if they had been honest, it would have then found its way to a lost property office somewhere. Either way, the connection with the dead girl was unlikely to be made. Once the right body was found, the rest was easy.

The Belmont party just happened to offer opportunity, but the truth was, there were always going to be parties and young men with cars available to a girl like Faun Moran and Vic had explored a number of options. It seemed like fate had a hand, though, when his most favoured one had presented itself.

Faun had played her part to perfection. She had made an already confused and woozy Mal Everson pull over into the trees on the edge of the Belmont estate. Vic had loaded the dead girl into the passenger seat of Mal's car and put Faun and the boy in the back of his. The girl's body had a silk scarf draped around the head and neck as though to protect the hair from being blown about. It also partly covered the face. Which was just as well, considering what the application of an iron bar had done to it. He had removed the body of the girl from the car before Faun had arrived, concealing it behind bushes and then ensured that Faun saw nothing of the dead woman.

Mal Everson was well out of it, Vic remembered. He remembered Faun Moran's face too as the reality of the situation suddenly hit home.

'I don't want to do this, Vic. I'm scared.'

'Too late to back out now, princess. You should always be careful what you wish for; didn't your mother ever tell you that?'

'But I thought you were funning. I didn't think you meant to do any of it.'

He had driven them to the chosen location, following Ben who was now driving Mal's car. Vic had parked some distance away and then, carrying the still unconscious Mal Everson, had gone to help Ben. Together they ensured the dead girl was securely pinioned in the seat and then removed the scarf. Vic remembered the shrill scream and realized that Faun must have followed after. She had, he realized, seen the mess he'd made of the head and neck. She had begun to scream, a shrill, frail sound, as though she'd been too shocked even to make a solid fist of that.

'Shut it,' Vic had told her. He poured petrol over the body and the seat and then handed her the can. She took it automatically, her fingers gripping but seemingly confused as to what she was holding. Her face was white, horrified.

The car had rolled easily. Ben and Vic thrust it over the lip of the gorge and watched, satisfied as it tumbled down the slope. Vic threw Mal's body after, then Ben had taken her arm, and holding her tightly so she could not run, he had led her back to his own car.

Then it was Vic's turn. The slope was steeper than he'd realized and twice he stumbled and rolled but he reached the bottom in one piece. The rest should have been easy. Light the girl's dress and let the flames destroy any evidence that this was not just an unfortunate accident with fatal results.

Standing back, out of harm's way, Vic had watched the fire take hold and for a wonderful, exhilarating moment he had told himself that they were home and dry.

And then he had heard voices.

Vic had never moved so fast, uphill, struggling against the brambles and the tree roots, but he made it.

He could hear the men struggling now to beat out the flames and knew it would be only a matter of time before the police arrived. He ventured to climb back on to the road only when he judged he was about a mile away.

Vic smiled, remembering. He'd felt euphoric, invincible, but not certain now that the deception would work; not knowing how much evidence the fire had destroyed. Reaching the car he found the girl in the front passenger seat, stunned and confused, a blossoming bruise on her chin.

'*She tried to shout when those others came,*' Ben told him. '*We couldn't have that, now could we?*'

'*You could have knocked me down with a feather,*' Vic told himself. *He recalled the moment he had realized that no one had questioned the identity of the girl in the car. Mal Everson apparently remembered nothing.*

'*Never know what you can do until you try,*' Vic told himself. '*You just never know.*'

NINETEEN

'I'm assuming you found nothing,' Henry said.

'Then you'd be assuming wrong, though how much, I don't know.' Mickey described the box and the lock. 'It was regularly maintained, and recently used, I would have said.' He showed Henry the handkerchief. 'Traces of a light oil,' he said. 'And there was this.' He waved the tiny twist of paper. 'A scrap of thread and a bead. I would be willing to bet that the dress Faun Moran was wearing on that beach had been in that box and this is a bead from it. But on its own it proves nothing.'

'No, it does not, though I suppose it's more than we had an hour ago. And I'm more convinced that Caxton is up to his neck in this business, as is Vic Mullins. The proving of it is another matter.'

When they arrived back in London they were told that Vic Mullins had been asking to see them and had been making a lot of noise about it. Henry decided that he could wait a little longer and went to speak to his superintendent about the possibility of getting a warrant, but it was in more hope than expectation and he was inevitably disappointed. A fragment of thread and one single bead was scant evidence. They might help to build a case, but they were not enough of a basis on which to search a man's house.

Henry went back to Central Office and was pleased to see that Mickey was brewing tea.

'No luck?'

'Of course not. Drink tea and then we'll see what Mr Mullins wants.' He checked the time. It was four in the afternoon. 'We will give him an hour, perhaps two, and then we will go home. If he has more to say then he can wait overnight and consider what he'd like to tell us.'

'We are being played, Henry. And the trouble is we don't know the rules of the game. But I have two more pieces of bad news, just to improve your afternoon. Pat phoned; she

does not recognize the handwriting. She thinks the contents
of the letters were florid and that Faun would have found them
dreadfully romantic, but has nothing more to add.'

Henry nodded. It had been something of a longshot anyway.
'And the other piece of bad news?'

'Our eyewitnesses in Bournemouth were shown a picture
of Vic Mullins but can't be sure that it was him. According
to the constable I spoke to, he thinks it might be, almost probably is, but they don't want to say a definite yes and get it
wrong. They reminded us that they did not see his face clearly,
just a figure on the beach.'

'The head and shoulders mugshot of a man they only saw
from a distance is not the best help. It gives you no sense of
size or scale. And they did not recognize him from the press
photograph we sent earlier, so . . .'

'And it is quite common for witnesses to become less certain
of a thing the more time that passes,' Mickey added. 'Perhaps
we could arrange for an identity parade.'

'If you can find a half-dozen men the size and shape of Vic
Mullins, then I'm very willing to countenance that.'

Mickey laughed. 'Yes, that would be a challenge. But I still
think it's something worth trying. I will ask the constables to
keep their eyes open for tall and broadly built men and we'll
see what we can do.'

'You are ever the optimist.'

'One of us has to be.'

'True. So let us see what Mr Mullins has to say now.'

They had Mullins brought into the same room as before, the
narrow window high up in the wall letting in very little light
and so late in the afternoon it was simply grey outside. The
single ball panning from the centre of the room seemed to
emphasize the darkness and the shadows and made an already
depressing room even more so. Mullins seemed unaffected by
that or by the news that the trunk had been empty.

'What trunk?' he asked.

'What do you mean what trunk. The trunk you told us about
yesterday, that was in your ex-employer's house in which you
say contained evidence. Though you never did tell us what
evidence.'

Vic's face was a picture of innocent disbelief. 'I don't know anything about a trunk.'

'I have it in my notes,' Mickey told him.

'Well, perhaps you wrote it down wrong. I don't recall telling you anything about a trunk. Why would I? What kind of trunk anyway?'

Mickey read back through his notes. 'A sixteenth-century, oak-carved trunk you claimed to be full of women's clothes. You claimed it to be evidence of crime and insisted that we went to look for it.'

'I think you are wrong. I never insisted on anything. How can I? You are the detectives. I am merely being detained.'

'I suppose you told us nothing about the car crash either,' Henry said. 'About how you staged this accident and how you procured the body that you intended to burn so that the world would believe that it was that of Faun Moran.'

'Well, from what I read in the newspaper accounts, the world did believe that it was Miss Moran. In that, of course, they were mistaken, but the world did believe it.'

'So what about this incident you gave evidence of yourself yesterday, about how you'd organized everything, procured the body, set the car ablaze.'

'So you must have spoken to Mr Caxton,' Vic said.

'We did, and he still tells us you are no longer in his employ and have not been for some time.'

'But did he also tell you that I was up with him in Yorkshire when the crash happened? Ah,' he said. 'I see from your faces that he did. So I could not have been at the crash, could I?'

'So why waste our time by telling us that you were?'

'Well, you see, there was this man. Paid me a good price to make up that story, said there would be a second payment in it for me.'

'What man?'

'Just some man in a pub. A gent he was, not a working man like me.'

'What work do you do?'

'Well, I did work for Mr Caxton, didn't I. Whatever Mr Caxton needed me to do and this man in the pub, he must have known that, because he came up to me and he said, Vic, I've got a little job for you, it would do no harm, because I know you weren't there. Mr Caxton can tell the police you weren't there, but I want you to tell them you were. See it as a favour, a paid for favour, you understand. Because a man like me, always needs a bit more money. So all I had to do was tell this yarn about the car crash, and about Miss Moran, and about the girl and go to you and tell you. Then all I had to do was endure a night or two in the cells, which is no great hardship. I knew you'd go and see Mr Caxton. I know Mr Caxton, even if we did have a bit of a falling out, I know that he would be honest enough to say where I was.'

'You expect us to believe that?'

'No matter if you believe it, can you prove it didn't happen? In my wallet you will find some money, a little bundle of five-pound notes which I will deposit in my bank when I get out of here. And I'm promised another little bundle of five-pound notes for my trouble.'

'And where are you supposed to collect this additional payment from?' Henry asked heavily.

'The man said he'd find me soon enough, and I believe he will. Perhaps in another pub.'

Henry had had enough. 'You're a liar, Mullins.'

'That might be true, but what am I lying about?' He asked as a broad grin spread across his face. The sense that this man had been enjoying himself had occurred to Henry right from the beginning, when Mullins had first sauntered into the police station.

'I suppose you weren't on the beach either,' Mickey said.

'Indeed I was not so. The same third party that gave me the money to say I was at the crash, gave me the money to say that too.'

'There were witnesses that say otherwise.'

'Then let the witnesses see me and say again that it was me. They were at some distance, gentlemen, I doubt they can be certain. A lawyer might argue that they could definitely not be certain at that distance. A lawyer might argue that if I can prove I was elsewhere then it was certainly not me on that beach.'

'Mr Caxton can't alibi you for that morning,' Mickey reminded him, 'because you were no longer in his employ.'

'Indeed I was not, but neither was I on the beach. I was up in Yorkshire with Mr Caxton when that car crash took place and I was in a boxing gym in Camden Town when that body was dumped on the beach. A bunch of us had been out the night before and were a little worse for wear, so we bunked down at the gym. It's an easy fact to check, Inspector. You speak to Mr Grady, that runs the gym, and he'll tell you I help out a lot, with the young fighters and that, and that we were celebrating a win. Four of us it was, we slept there, and woke up with thick heads in the morning. So you see, I have an alibi for that one too. You gentlemen will no doubt check out my alibis and you will then charge me with wasting police time, and I will no doubt go down for a week or two or whatever the magistrate decides, but I will have my little bundle of fivers and then my other little bundle of fivers to help me through the experience.'

Vic was taken back to his cell. A telegraph was sent to the local police and they sent a messenger to the gymnasium in Camden Town. A couple of hours later they had the confirmation. Yes, Mr Mullins had been there when he said he had been. Yes, they were celebrating a win, and if Detective Chief Inspector Johnstone cared to look at the back pages of the local paper on 5 January, they could read all about it. Mr Mullins was an invaluable help at their gymnasium.

'So that's that then,' Henry said. 'Where do we go from here? We both know he's now lying and that the alibis are false. That both Vic Mullins and Caxton are playing us for fools, playing games at our expense.'

'We do our best to break the lies they're telling us,' Mickey said. 'There will be gaps somewhere that we can lever open, you can be sure of that.'

'Right now I'm not sure of anything. Let's go home, Mickey, and sleep on it.'

'What we can do,' Mickey said, 'is take a trip round the mortuaries and find out if a young woman did go missing about the time of the car crash.'

'That's if she was taken from a London mortuary.'

'It's a place to start, and there are several in London, the numbers are not so great in the provincial towns, and young people go missing here every day of the week and turn up dead in unfortunate circumstances. It will be something to do tomorrow, so I intend to do it.'

Henry nodded. 'It's as good a place to start as any,' he agreed.

Vic

He remembered driving Faun from the scene, and Ben telling her that she was safe now, that no one could find her, that no one knew where she was and seeing the look in her eyes as she realized just how deep in she was, and that the water was closing over her head. That she was drowning.

'Let me go,' she begged him. 'Just let me go, just let me out anywhere. I won't tell what happened. I'll say that I stumbled away from the crash and didn't know where I was and that I have no idea about that girl in the car, that maybe we gave her a lift. I'll make up some kind of story and, no one will know. You can't do this to me. I know you like me and I can be nice to you.'

Ben had reached across to the passenger seat and patted her knee. 'It's a little late for that,' he told her. 'But just let this game play out. I'm told you Bright Young Things like games.'

He could see that she was appalled and shocked. 'This isn't a game. This isn't a scavenger hunt or a race across town. That girl was dead.'

'Of course she was, I wouldn't want to put a living girl in the car and then roll it down the hill and set fire to her. Don't you worry about that – she was dead long before I put her in that car. Dead and forgotten about in some mortuary in east London. No one had come to claim her. Don't you worry about that.'

She touched the jaw where he had thumped her, not hard enough to break it, but hard enough to put her out cold for a while. Ben, like Vic, had long since learnt to control the forces of his strike. When to hit an opponent just hard enough that they go down but not out, when to prolong the fight, when to finish it. 'You'll be bruised for a while,' he said, 'but no damage done. Maybe a loose tooth or two, but leave them alone and they'll settle down.'

'You've never cared about me, have you?'

'I like you just fine.'

'Did you ever care about me? You wrote me all those letters.' She sounded hopeful.

'I don't imagine anyone will know that, even if they find them. When my right hand was hurt, I learned to write with my left. I'm now perfectly capable of writing with my right and doing most things with my right, but it's still useful to use my left on occasions. Such as when I want to disguise my handwriting. Did you never notice that the handwriting on the letters was different from my usual hand? Or were you just so preoccupied by all that adoration and all that flowery language?'

Vic remembered the look in her eyes, the utter despair, the betrayal and almost, almost he felt sorry for her. Just for an instant he wondered about stopping the car and letting her out, but then the impulse passed. He felt in his pocket for the hip flask and passed it over to her. 'Here, have a swig of this. It will ease the pain in your poor jaw.'

She was so eager for even a glimpse of kindness that she took it and took a few sips. It was enough – within minutes she was drifting into unconsciousness. He reached and took the flask back before she dropped it and replaced it in his pocket. They would be driving through more populated areas and they could do without her screaming or shouting out. She would sleep now until they reached the Caxton house, after which she would no longer be a problem.

TWENTY

Faun, December

I have sent my letter. Martha took it from me when she came to say goodbye. She begged to be able to make that one final visit to me, saying that she would miss 'her lady' as she has come to call me. I'm going to miss her so much. She was the only kind person left in my world and I'm so afraid that she will be unable to deliver my message. More scared that she merely humoured me and that she will give it to HIM. After all, he is all sweetness and light to her.

Though I expect I will soon know if that is the case. He will punish me for it. I'm afraid of what he will do. He's done so much to hurt me already. He tells me that we will still be man and wife, that he's moulding me ready for the role, that he doesn't want a wife that answers back.

I will kill myself first. I have the means. I broke that brittle glass slide of his and if I have to then I will use that but I won't surrender to him.

Pat, please come and find me. Please come and fetch me home. I can't bear to think that you might not get my letter. I have to try and stay alive until you come. Pat, my darling sister, please come for me.

Wednesday 22 January into Thursday 23 January

The call had gone out to all hospital mortuaries, undertakers and anywhere else where a body might conceivably be stored or from which a body might conceivably be lost. Mickey did not have a lot of hope regarding this undertaking but by Wednesday evening they had a handful of possible responses, one of which looked particularly promising.

On the Thursday morning, almost three weeks after Faun

Moran's body had been discovered on the beach, Mickey went to speak to his contact at St Thomas's Hospital. A young woman had been brought in, some three days before the car crash in Derbyshire. She had been knocked down by a car, but what had killed her was the fall not the car itself.

'She had an unusually thin skull, just one of those things. She hit the kerbstone at an oblique angle and she was dead.'

The accident had not happened locally to St Thomas's, but as they happened to have capacity that was where the body had been sent. Her identity was unknown but a photograph had been taken in the hope that relatives might eventually be reunited with the girl and a list of her belongings had been made.

'The day following her death both she and her possessions disappeared. At first it was thought she had just been moved to a different hospital. That perhaps she had been identified and the family had made other arrangements, but then it was realized that she was nowhere to be found. The man on night duty was questioned and found to have been drunk though he swears that nobody came down to the mortuary while he was there, and swears also he would have heard them. He was dismissed, of course – no one seems to know of his whereabouts now. This is his name and last known address, and any details that could be gleaned about him from other members of staff, but I'm afraid I can't be much more help.'

Mickey took his prizes back to Scotland Yard to share with Henry. 'She looks nothing like Miss Moran, but from what we know of the height and build of both young women there would have been enough of a similarity. The hair colouring is the same and of a similar length. We know from the post-mortem that she was beaten severely around the face and head, thankfully after her death, and for the purposes of misdirection. I still believe that a proper post-mortem would have revealed that this was not Faun, but without that it's not so unexpected or unexplained that mistakes were made.'

'In that I think you're being too generous,' Henry told him. 'However, at least we know that there was a body stolen from the mortuary, so perhaps we should present this to Mr Mullins and see what happens.'

Vic was duly brought upstairs from the cells back into the interview room. Henry laid the photograph of the unknown girl on the desk and Vic Mullins looked at it.

'And who is this?'

'It's the girl you took from the mortuary at St Thomas's. How much did you pay the attendant to look the other way? Or did you just buy him the alcohol and let nature take its course?'

'And I'm supposed to understand what you're on about? I told you, I just spun you a yarn and I never said I took anybody from a mortuary. So when are you going to let me out of here?'

'When I'm satisfied. So prepare yourself for a long wait.'

'What do you intend to charge me with? Look, Chief Inspector, I have been a very patient man, but I came in here and made a voluntary statement so under the judges' rules you should have released me long ago. Not questioned me further on subjects that were not mentioned within my statement.'

'A statement which you have since changed.'

'But still made voluntarily. You didn't arrest me – I came here on my own two feet. So I suggest you let me walk out on those same two feet. I will be making a complaint.'

'You were cautioned, you made a statement. You have wasted police time.'

'So charge me or let me out of here. My alibis stand up, don't they?'

'He's right,' Mickey said when he took a few moments out to discuss the matter with Henry. 'I'm only surprised he hasn't pressed this before. As to his alibis, his ex-employer is rich enough to have bought silence or collaboration. The story of them being in Yorkshire is proving hard to check, as you know. They were registered at the hotel Caxton named, but who knows if they stayed there at all times? According to Caxton, they went walking. It's a place popular with walkers and fishermen and others of irregular habits who don't necessarily return for dinner. And Mullins is right. We have gone beyond the bounds, Henry. While our superintendent has granted us some latitude, I imagine his patience will also be wearing thin.'

'So we let him go, and we have him followed, and we see what he does next.'

An hour later and Vic Mullins was on his way. Those following him reported that he had gone to his lodgings, and that was, it seemed, where he stayed.

The following morning Henry discovered that he was once more the subject of newspaper reports. Not the hero this time but the officer who had arrested an innocent man who had come to make what he thought was going to be a helpful statement to the police – voluntarily and on his own two feet – but who had been cautioned and locked in a cell and questioned repeatedly, despite this being contrary to accepted practice and regulation.

'They're making a meal of this,' Mickey said. 'But how did they get these facts in time for the early edition? Mullins had no visitors when he was here, and as far as we know he sent no message out.'

'So the report was issued from elsewhere but no doubt concocted with Mullins' cooperation and dictation. His own two feet indeed.'

Henry tossed the newspaper he had been reading back on the stack. He was beginning to feel as though it'd been a mistake to come back to work. He could have used his time better elsewhere and to better effect. He was making no headway here. He felt his efforts to have been clumsy, ineffectual. He didn't blame the newspapers for their change of tune.

'He will slip up, Henry,' Mickey told him. 'And so will Ben Caxton, and we will have both of them together.'

Vic had left his lodgings by the rear exit and walked to the lock-up garage where his car was parked and then he had driven back to his employer's house.

Ben was in his sitting room and Vic sat down beside the fire and watched as Ben poured them both a drink.

'It will be good to sleep the night in a proper bed,' Vic said.

Ben raised a glass as a toast to his friend. 'But you must keep no more souvenirs,' Ben told him. 'And we must wait a while for the fuss to die down before it's time for the next game to begin.'

'And with a more satisfactory ending the next time,' Vic told him. 'No foolish accidents.'

Vic

She had asked if she could have a bath and Ben had obliged, bringing her downstairs into his own bathroom. Vic could see that she was even more unsettled, her eyes bright and feverish and she had grown unpredictable and so he was not totally surprised when she threw herself at Ben, hands like claws, going for his eyes.

But her feet were wet and the tiled floor was slippery, and as she lurched forward Vic had made a grab at her and as she swivelled, trying to push him away, her feet had slid. Angrily Ben had kicked out, bringing her down heavily, and she had hit her head on the side of the marble bath and then lay very still.

'You killed her.'

'She killed herself. She slipped and fell and killed herself.' He bent and touched her head. Her neck was twisted at an odd angle and it was evident that it was broken.

Vic recalled the disappointment on his employer's face. Ben had not done with her yet. When he had tired of his women he liked to end things himself, deliberately, not have some accident take that pleasure from him.

'Get rid of her,' Ben had said. He stood up and for a moment looked down on the woman with something like pity and then the look was gone, the hardness was back in his eyes and when he strode away there was no grief in his body. It was as though she had already been forgotten. Vic, as he had done so many times before, prepared to clean up.

The game was over. It would be a little while before Ben was ready for the new one to begin. But it would, Vic thought. There would always be another game.

TWENTY-ONE

I t was early February when something happened that completely changed the direction of the investigation. An investigation that had largely been set aside. Hot on the heels of Vic Mullins' complaints in the press came a more measured but even more virulent protest from Ben Caxton who revealed that he had been a suspect in the disappearance and murder of Faun Moran. He had been questioned by the police but they had found no evidence because there had been none to find. He said in his statement released to the press that he understood the police must follow every lead but that he had expected them to do it with a little more grace. He had found Detective Chief Inspector Henry Johnstone to be rude and surly and could not help but wonder if Inspector Johnstone's recent personal trials might have left their mark.

Slow burning anger impacted on every aspect of Henry Johnstone's life in those weeks. He knew he was unbearable to live with, to work with, just to be around, but he could not seem to help himself. He knew Caxton was guilty, Vic Mullins too, but he had been instructed to let things lie and that he had no real option in the matter.

On the fourth of February he received a phone call from Patricia Clifford, Faun's older sister. Her news was strange.

'I received the oddest and most disturbing of letters in the post this morning and I think you should see it. It was from Faun and it was written to me just a few days before Christmas. It arrived in a cheap envelope, and the address was in a very childish hand. It was written on what looks like a folded piece of butcher's paper but it is undoubtedly from her.'

She sounded broken, but at the same time could not keep the excitement out of her voice.

'What does it say?' Henry asked.

'In brief, that she was being held against her will by Ben Caxton and she was asking someone called Martha, a very

young maidservant from the sound of it, to post this letter
letting me know where she was and begging me to come and
rescue her. Henry, imagine. She must've been waiting all over
Christmas and into New Year. She must've believed herself
abandoned.'

'And why has it taken so much time to reach you?'

'That I don't know, but I know where this young girl can
be found. She apparently told Faun that she was going to be
in service to some people down in Kent, people called
the Philpots. So Faun must have given her this letter and for
some reason she didn't post it until now.'

'Caxton will say that it's a forgery.'

'I know my sister's handwriting. And besides she says there
is evidence hidden in the room where she was kept. She kept
some kind of written record and she hid the fragments of paper
in the wainscot, there was a crack. She knew that she could
not remove these pieces of paper without smashing the wainscot but she wanted to leave something behind in the hope
that it would help punish the guilty. Henry, she knew that it
was almost certain she would die if I didn't come and rescue
her. Oh my poor baby sister, what she must have gone through.'

'Pat, you have told no one else about this?'

'Only Violet. I would have told my husband but he's away.
Violet won't say anything, you know that. We are motoring
up to London this morning and will be with you soon. Henry,
please say that this is going to be all right. That you will be
able to charge them this time.'

'I let you down. I'm sorry.'

'There will be nothing to be sorry for. Not if you can act
now. Henry, don't take this the wrong way, but you came up
against a man cleverer than you, more conscienceless and
cruel. You were behaving in your usual honest manner, perhaps
that was not enough.'

'So what now?' Mickey asked. 'Henry, this is the break-
through we've needed. Now we must find the girl and discover
why she only just sent the letter and we must get a search
warrant. They will grant it this time.'

Henry picked up the telephone.

'Who are you calling?'

'Mr Caius Moran. And I'm going to suggest that he kicks up the biggest stink he can if a warrant isn't issued. He can drag all our names through the mud, if that's what it takes. He can phone every newspaper in London, Mickey, I don't care anymore. I will not be beaten. The dead women deserve justice and I will do whatever is required to ensure they get it.'

A couple of hours later they were on the train heading for Kent, knowing that back in London warrants were being prepared. Henry wanted everything in place, every fragment of knowledge he could get before going to the Caxton house once more. Briefly, he had spoken to Pat and read the letter when she had arrived at Scotland Yard, and then handed her over to his superintendent. She had spoken to her father and for once the two of them were in total agreement. They would, he reckoned, make a formidable pair.

Henry had been to Kent once before; he knew that the entire constabulary owned only the one car and so he had made no attempt to get a police driver, but declared that they would hire a taxi at the station, and Pat had pressed money on him saying that they had no idea quite how far away the Philpot house might be. He had not called ahead, just in case they should contact Ben Caxton. With luck, the arrest of Ben Caxton and Vic Mullins would happen more or less at the same time as they reached the Philpots and Henry had asked that the search not be made until he could return. He could allow others to make the arrests but did not feel that he could bear to be absent from that final discovery.

The Philpot house was a red-brick affair, not large or grand but more like an overgrown farmhouse. It felt friendly as did Mrs Philpot and Henry had a hard time understanding that her family were genuine friends of Caxton's. But then he reminded himself that the man could be charming when it suited him.

Mrs Philpot was puzzled, but she called Martha from the kitchen and told her that the gentlemen were police officers but that she was not in any trouble. Martha, Henry suddenly realized, was indeed just a child. A little slip of a girl who burst into tears at the sight of the police officers and said she

was 'Sorry,' but the lady had said no one must handle the
letter except for Martha, and she must be the one to post it
and she'd had no opportunity.

'But Martha, you know that the post is taken from here
once a day, that Miles takes it. If you had a letter to post he
could have taken it for you.'

'The lady was frightened, and she was so unwell, I didn't
know she ever would be well again. Mr Caxton was meant to
be looking after her, but the lady said that she wanted to go
home. She asked me specially if I would post this letter, but
I didn't get a day off, not till the day before yesterday,
when I had a half day and I went into town. I walked all the
way there and all the way back. I promised the young lady
that I would post the letter, and not give it to anyone else. Did
I do wrong, sir?'

'You did your best,' Mickey said gently. 'Now we need you
to sit down and write everything you remember about this
young lady and the circumstances of how you met her.
Everything you can think about, you understand?'

'My writing's ain't so good, sir. But I'll do my best. I'm
not in trouble with you, am I, ma'am?'

'No, I'm certain you're not. Martha, Cook will help you, I
will make sure of that later. You can tell her what you need
to put and she will help you set the words down.'

Martha was dismissed, still obviously distressed.

'Now I want to know what's going on.'

'First I need to use your telephone,' Henry told her.

'Very well, if you must. But I deserve an explanation.'

She did indeed, Henry thought, but she was not going to
like it one little bit.

An hour later they were back at the railway station, Mrs Philpot
having allowed the use of her car and driver to get back there.
They had briefly outlined the story and she had declared herself
unconvinced but Henry could see that there was something at
the back of her mind that made her wonder.

'I've been reading all about this in the newspapers,' she
told him. 'I must say I don't think you've acquitted yourself
particularly well.'

'I'm hoping to do better now,' Henry told her.

Later, much later, after a train journey, and what felt like an age by car, they were once more at the Caxton residence but this time all of the lights were on, and there were police cars in front of the house.

'So, where do we begin?' Henry wondered.

'In that study of his, opening that hidden door on the wall opposite the little office. I'll wager that's where she was kept. And I'll wager that Clarke knows how to open it. And that he'd rather open it than have us break it down.'

In the room above the study there was a narrow bed, a table and a wooden chair. Barred windows suggested it had once been a nursery but there was nothing of childhood or play in this space now. Henry was reminded of the bedroom at the top of a tall house where Melissa had been held prisoner before being taken to the damp, dark cellar where Henry had eventually found her. This space was not damp, but neither was it warm. The fireplace didn't look as though it had been used in a long time. There was no comfort here.

The room was panelled in scuffed, dark wood and there, beside the bed, was a panel with a long, narrow crack as had been described in the letter. Henry could imagine the despair of the girl imprisoned here. She could stand on the bed and see out of the window but the rest of the house would have been totally cut off, all sound deadened, all sense of human contact removed.

Apart from little Martha. And she, as Mickey had said, had done her best. Though it transpired her best had probably only increased the agony as Faun waited for her sister to come and find her. Did she think . . . she must have thought, as Pat had said, that she had been utterly abandoned.

'Help me pull the bed away from the wall.'

'There are scratches on the floor and a broken microscope slide,' Mickey said. He knelt to examine them. 'She must have tried to keep track of the days. Poor little scrap. There are pencil shavings too and scrapings of the lead. Henry, I think she used that bit of glass to sharpen the point. So where did she hide the pencil and the paper?'

Henry pulled the thin, flock mattress from the bedframe.

She had cut a small slit with the glass and concealed her precious pencil and paper inside. But clearly she had desired a safer spot for her writing.

Taking out his penknife, Henry slid it into the crack in the timber and levered a section free. The wood splintered and gave way with a loud snap. Behind the panel were a dozen or so slips of paper. Some the size of his hand, some larger, obviously torn from sections of butcher's paper; Martha must have saved the unstained sections. There were also two flimsy sheets of cheap writing paper, carefully detached from a pad. The glue still visible at one edge. They were covered in writing, words packed close and small. She had covered every available space.

'Martha tried to do her best to help,' Mickey said. 'But the poor chick must have felt her loyalties divided between what she perceived as a kind master and a sick woman in need of compassion.' He paused, then asked softly, 'What do you think they did to her up here?'

'The post-mortem told a story of rape and abuse, Mickey, even if the surgeon chose to couch his report in gentler terms.'

Henry sat with his back against the panelled wall and began to read. He skimmed the first three pages and then handed the whole stack to Mickey as though he could not bear to examine the rest. 'But we have them now, Mickey. Alibis or not, we have them both.'

Epilogue

' I wish we could provide her with a headstone. A proper one bearing her name and age and not just the date of her death,' Cynthia said.

'One day we might discover who she was,' Mickey told her. 'At least she now has a proper grave in a proper graveyard, and if we ever find her family we can bring them here.'

Cynthia nodded. A great many strings had been pulled to allow this to happen and Cynthia had willingly footed the bill. The girl from the car, once mistaken for Faun Moran, now had a final resting place.

The funeral had been a small affair. Mickey and Belle, Henry and his sister and Pat and Violet, two young women he had come to admire.

'Did you ever discover what happened to the photographs?' Cynthia asked curiously. 'From the crash site?'

'Mickey did. He spent some time looking through the files of various investigations that Shelton had worked on and it seems that in a fit of pique the man had muddled evidence and no doubt destroyed more before he left under his self-made cloud. There will be a disciplinary hearing. But those particular photographs still have not turned up. It's likely they never will.'

'That's appalling, Henry.'

'It is, and most likely it would not have been discovered if Faun Moran had not suddenly reappeared.'

Cynthia gripped his arm sympathetically. 'It all turned out well,' she said.

'And how is your brother?' Henry asked Violet as they walked from the grave.

'Improving with every day. I think a weight of guilt was lifted, but then replaced by another, less definable sense of responsibility. But he is coming to terms with the idea that he was the dupe in this and there was nothing he could have done. I hope he will be home again before the summer. I'm planning a trip abroad, Paris, perhaps and I'd like to take him with me. Our father approves; I think he's hoping to keep the pair of us out of mischief.'

'In Paris?'

'Well, maybe just out of the public eye. We all owe you a great debt, Henry.'

He shook his head. 'I think I made rather a mess of things, at least at first.'

They reached her car and paused. 'What makes someone do what they did? I can't understand it. They must have known that it was wrong, morally degenerate and yet they seem not to have given a damn.'

'Perhaps some men are simply born that way. Though I do believe that alone neither Vic Mullins nor Ben Caxton would have gone so far. They seemed to feed, one from the other, to support a common purpose. An evil purpose, certainly.'

'Well, I hope I never understand,' Violet said emphatically. 'I don't want to be able to comprehend the minds of people who can treat others with such cruelty. And poor Faun was not the only victim, was she?'

'It would seem not. They claim that there were others, but there's no proof we can lay hands on. It might just all be talk. Caxton speaks about their activities as a game, a challenge. I've no doubt they derived all kinds of amusement from having Mullins come and make his statement and send us skittering about like mice, just to withdraw it again.'

It still rankled, this feeling that they had just been used like toys in another's game. But, Henry thought, that didn't really matter when offered up against the suffering of Faun Moran and the other women. And he had no doubt but there were other women.

And one day, he promised, he would discover all of their names.